KU-335-335

Iain McDowall was born in Kilmarnock, Scotland. He worked as a philosophy lecturer and as a computing specialist before turning to crime (writing). Currently, he divides his time between Crowby and his home in Cheltenham. *A Study In Death* is the first in a series of novels featuring Chief Inspector Jacobson and DS Kerr. For further details visit www.crowby.co.uk

A Study In Death

Iain McDowall

PIATKUS

For more information on other books
published by Piatkus, visit our website at
www.piatkus.co.uk

First published in Great Britain in 2000 by
Judy Piatkus (Publishers) Ltd of
5 Windmill Street, London W1T 2JA
email:info@piatkus.co.uk

The moral right of the author has been asserted

*A catalogue record for this book is available from the British
Library*

ISBN 0 7499 3211 2

Set in Times by
Action Publishing Technology Ltd, Gloucester

Printed and bound in Great Britain by
Mackays of Chatham plc, Chatham, Kent

For Rory . . . on a magic night

Thursday

Chapter One

In the Beginning

There were two possibilities available. He could roll over and contain his anger until sleep came or he could persist and provoke her into a further outburst of emotion. He decided to try for sleep. He pulled the duvet with him as he turned away. It was a final provocation but she refused to react, clung firmly to her pillow. A filmic image came to him, the camera panning down from a highpoint on the opposite side of the room: two reclining figures in an intimate landscape of bedclothes and unresolved rage.

He was shouting at both his mother and his father when the ugly purr of the telephone finally woke him from his troubled dreams. Beside him, Cathy muttered something indecipherable and immediately fell back to sleep.

'Jacobson here, Ian. There's a dead body that shouldn't be and we're both on the case. I'll be addressing the assembled masses in half an hour.'

Jacobson didn't waste any words, stayed on the phone just long enough to attain his yawning assent. Kerr couldn't remember when he'd drifted off, hoped he'd grabbed enough sleep to see him through the day. His legs found the carpet and his automatic pilot steered him into the bathroom. Ten minutes: he pissed, slapped cold, then hottish, then too hot water on his face, endured the misery of a half-asleep shave. He moved quietly back into the bedroom, pulled on his clothes without disturbing his wife. From the doorway, he looked back at the bed. Only her sleeping, sleepy head was visible, her face blondly obscured by her hair.

I love you. He said it out loud, knowing she wouldn't hear, made his way downstairs with quiet footsteps. In the front room he switched on the light. The stain of spilt Chianti on the couch had dried from red to brown, uprooted books and records were still strewn everywhere. The crack across the front of the television set looked far worse than it had seemed the night before. He left the debris where it was and went out into the hall. There were a couple of envelopes on the doormat, almost certainly bills. He picked them up and carried them through to the kitchen table, ignoring the cat's plaintive meowing from the other side of the front door. If he didn't have time for breakfast himself then there was no reason why she couldn't wait either.

*

Detective Sergeant Ian Kerr settled down on the back row of the briefing room. It was standard modern practice for the duty soco to video the crime scene on arrival. Somebody dimmed the lights and the latest snuff movie began: the body of a man about five feet ten, thin, face down, blue 501s and a green check shirt. The scalpline was matted with black coagulated blood which spread down and outwards so that the corpse seemed to be floating on a dense, black puddle. Black insects buzzed silently on the screen.

When the lights came back on, a burly figure stood up at the front of the room. Detective Chief Inspector Frank Jacobson coughed smokily, unhealthily, before speaking.

'The victim is likely to be identified as Roger Harvey, age thirty-six, university lecturer, not married, not known as a homosexual or a drug user, no criminal record. No obvious motive, in short, to bash his brains into mashed potato.'

Jacobson paused for effect. Kerr glanced discreetly at his watch. It was seven thirty-seven am.

'Chummie says he found the body around four o'clock. Once we know the likeliest time of death we should be able to eliminate him provided he can account for his whereabouts. In the meantime we'll hold on to him but provisionally it looks as if we're buying his story:

5

a well-dead stiff discovered in the course of breaking and entering.'

Kerr and Jacobson followed the custody sergeant along the corridor in the direction of the interview rooms.

'So Geordie's really in the clear?'

'He's a stupid bugger, but harmful to himself alone. Pure panic reaction. Undoubtedly attributes magic powers to the forensics. Assumed that somehow there'd be a trace of him when we finecombed the premises so he runs straight down the local nick with the news. Actually, it might be an idea if you do the business on your own. Just run him through his statement again. There might be some detail or other he's forgotten to mention. That way I'll have time to call in on Merchant, see what's shaping up in the pathology lab. Tell McCulloch we expect to bail him on the burglary charge as soon as the time of death's confirmed. The last bloody thing we need is another junkie topping himself in the cells.'

The custody sergeant opened the door and Jacobson peered in with the air of a master of ceremonies.

'Cheer up, Geordie. I've brought an old pal to see you.'

George McCulloch's fingers drummed the table. He looked up impassively, watched Kerr sit down.

'Hello Geordie. I was really sorry to hear about Sylvie.'

'Ah know that, Mr Kerr, but wance yer oan that stuff . . .'

His thin voice trailed off. There was no need in any case to complete this statement of the obvious. Together Sylvie and George had carried out a fairly impressive series of small-scale cons, credit card rip-offs and the occasional old-fashioned burglary. Like a schoolteacher or a doctor, Kerr thought, you always remember those first cases, almost felt a soft spot for them. At their second or third arrest, Kerr, newly out of uniform and keen, had talked the McCullochs into a methadone programme, kept them from a stretch. Now she was dead from adulterated gear and he'd just done the flat of a murder victim.

Kerr read McCulloch's statement over to him again. He asked him to re-tell the crucial parts of his version of events once, twice, even three times. But there were no flaws, no obvious inconsistencies. He was either telling the whole truth or lying skilfully from start to finish.

'You're absolutely sure there's nothing you saw or heard that you haven't mentioned? If we could clear this up quickly—'

'Ah'm sure, Mr Kerr.'

He offered and lit McCulloch a cigarette from the pack which, as a non-smoker, he carried solely for professional reasons. He could have hated himself for that 'quickly', for its easy, dishonest implication. McCulloch would go down this time even if he came up with the killer's name, address and hat size inside the next three seconds. There was nothing useful for Kerr to do here but a minute still passed in uneasy silence before he spoke again.

'OK. That's it for now. The autopsy and first lab reports should be through by tonight. If it all checks out, we won't oppose bail. The constable will take you back to the cell when you've finished your smoke.'

Kerr slid the cigarette packet across the table as he stood up. McCulloch tried a smile as slight as his huddled frame, as slender as his future.

Professor Alasdair Merchant's office was separate from the morgue itself. Like most policemen who had been in the vicinity of a mortuary more than once, Jacobson was quite happy to wait until Merchant had time to see him rather than to insist on interrupting him at his work. He found himself yawning as he sat there, suddenly hit by the fatigue of a morning which already seemed several hours too long.

He got up and poured himself a plastic cupful of coffee from Merchant's filter machine, struggling with the simultaneous temptation to light up another cigarette. It really was time to knock the habit on the head, he told himself. Ditto booze, ditto microwaved pub meals, ditto late night Baltis, ditto insufficient exercise. Keep this up and in a year or two he'd be back here on a slab of his own, his wrecked body providing more raw material for Merchant's highly regarded research.

It was hardly Merchant's fault that his career, unlike Jacobson's, had been a dazzling success. Nor was Merchant responsible for the fact that his tall, straight frame always forced Jacobson into an unwelcome comparison with his own physical state. The same was true of the permanent tan which resulted from his frequent invitations to conferences in Orlando or Madrid or Hawaii. But Jacobson didn't dislike him any less because his dislike was irrational. Glancing around him, he noticed that at least the health advice posters with their rotted lungs and diseased livers had finally disappeared. In their place was a full-size cinema poster in an expensive-looking frame. *Belle de Jour* was the title of the film. Jacobson had never heard of it, although he thought the starring actress's name sounded familiar. It was probably the kind of thing that Janice used to watch late at night after he'd given up on another of their failed evenings together. After he'd crawled off to bed on his own, neither as drunk nor as oblivious as he would have chosen to be.

The crime scene was a nondescript block of flats, six floors high, on the edge of town. Kerr slowed to a crawl as the block came into view at the end of a winding street of semis. The area was close to the countryside but not close enough. The relentless line of electricity pylons, which stretched out into the surrounding hills, grabbed the eyes far more than the hills themselves. Entry-level suburbia: you lived here if you were straight enough to qualify for a mortgage but still only a joke punter in the real property stakes. Office fodder, nine to five, computers, sales, teachers and – no doubt – coppers. What his father would have called Thatcher's children, willingly or unwillingly intent on keeping the wolf from their doors, their heads above the gutter.

A car park with numbered spaces filled the void between the block and the closest semi. He parked up alongside a couple of patrol cars and got out into a strong November wind. At the far end of the car park, a young constable stood watchfully beside a blue Peugeot 205, the car, Kerr surmised, which must have belonged to the victim. Inside the first-floor flat where the murder had taken place, he found the soco still hard at work and not exactly overjoyed by his interruption.

Roger Harvey's flat was small and neatly but sparsely furnished if you excluded the massive amount of books and papers which it contained. A lounge, bedroom, kitchen, bathroom and narrow hall with only the latter two devoid of bookshelves filled to capacity. The far side of the lounge, nearest the window, evidently doubled as a study. Here more piles of books jostled for floorspace with bulging folders of various styles and ages and an old dining table bore the weight of a personal computer, printer and yet more books and papers. If the case turned slow, there would be a massive amount of sifting and delving to undertake.

He tried to fix the detail of the room in his memory. A long grey sofa marked the start of what was presumably the lounging part of the lounge: tv, video and a high quality set of hi-fi separates. They would have made Geordie's week if it hadn't been for the stiff. To one side of a fireplace with an unlit gas fire at its centre, the bottom row of shelving contained the dead man's records, cassettes, cds. Moving carefully, Kerr crossed the room and stood between the sofa and the fire from where he could make out the record which lay on the Linn deck. The stylus was still halfway across the surface. He strained his neck to read the label – *Astral Weeks*, Van Morrison. Kerr wondered when the music had stopped and under what circumstances, whether it had been the victim or the murderer or an innocent third party who had switched it off. At least, he thought, there was a possibility that Harvey had gone out to a decent soundtrack.

The soco had been dusting for fingerprints by the window sill all this while but now it looked as if he was about to start on the area around the fireplace. Kerr decided not to push his luck any further. The detailed searching through Harvey's possessions would have to wait, as properly he knew it should, until after the soco's work was done.

'Inspector Jacobson should be here any minute. I think I'll wait outside for him. I wouldn't want to get in your way.'

Jacobson drove out past the perimeter of the hospital towards the bypass, Crowby's quarter-inch of the motorway map. Fast access to the suburbs when – a standard Jacobsonism – it wasn't clogged up like a free night in a brothel. He accelerated out of the slipway, entered the first lane ahead – just – of a thundering lorry. The driver's horn and flashing headlamps communicated his opinion of the manoeuvre. Jacobson, lost in irascible thoughts, didn't appear to notice.

His detour to the hospital had been close enough to a complete waste of time. Merchant, when he'd finally put in an appearance, had added virtually nothing to the picture which his assistant, Robinson, called out to the crime scene in the early hours, had already painted. Fatal blows to the head and a lot of them: 'Many blows beyond the point necessary to bring about death.' The inexperienced Robinson had indicated that the victim must have been dead for at least a couple of days. Merchant had been slightly more expansive: 'three, or more likely, four days.' But that had been that: 'There's really nothing more I can tell you, Inspector, before the autopsy is carried out.'

For these jewels, he'd had to endure the healthy glow of the taut, tanned face, the flashing smile of Merchant's perfect nicotine-free teeth. The offended trucker caught up, passed, a hand like a shovel wasting a v-sign on Jacobson's non-registering brain. It was no good: the more he tried to ignore the impulse, the more his mind kept circling back to it. He'd only had one all morning. Another one, he lied to himself, would not hurt.

Anwar Ahmed was in a hurry but eager to help the police. Jacobson, Kerr and Ahmed made up a semi-circle of figures as they sat on Ahmed's brown sofa and chairs around a glass-topped coffee table in a second-floor lounge. On the first floor, directly under their feet, was the spot where Harvey's life had ebbed away.

'I must meet a client in thirty minutes. I had to call back for some papers. You want tea?'

Kerr looked open to persuasion but Jacobson shook his head.

'No thanks, Mr Ahmed. We don't want to keep you longer than necessary. Did you know Roger Harvey at all?'

'By sight only. He was a quiet man, I think. Occasionally, I would see him in the hall and say hello. I recognised him from my time at the university. I thought at first he was a student for he was always dressed scruffy, jeans and so on. Then one time, my sister is visiting and she told me he was a lecturer.'

'She knew him?'

'Not really, I don't think. But she studied English Literature, so naturally she knew who the lecturers were in that faculty.'

Jacobson studied Ahmed's elegant suit, the silk waistcoat he was wearing under the jacket. Before him on the table the tools of his trade were contained inside a smart executive case. Ahmed fidgeted with his mobile phone, anxious to be going. On the other side of the room, his wife was changing their baby's nappy with the result that the conversation was punctuated by infant gurgling.

'So a quiet man – and a quiet neighbour?'

'Oh yes. Not like us I fear.'

Ahmed nodded in the direction of the mother and the baby.

'Occasionally some music and laughter late at night. Part of life, isn't it? Only exception was Sunday night, funnily enough.'

'This Sunday?'

'Yes, late too. Around one in the morning. I was taking my turn with my daughter and I heard loud, angry voices. Next thing, the door slammed. I thought I heard some noises after that, like bangings. Then there was silence.'

'Could you hear what was said? Did it go on for long?'

'No, only that the tone was angry. Sunila was wailing, so I could not hear clearly. It did not last long – five, ten minutes.'

'How many—'

'Two main voices and a third which I think was perhaps a woman. I cannot be sure.'

'Mrs Ahmed, did—'

'Yes, I heard them too but also not clearly. Two or three voices. They went on for maybe five minutes – then silence.'

Jacobson handed the about-to-be unpunctual accountant a card.

'Thank you both for your help. An officer may contact you in the next couple of days to take a formal note of what you've told us. In the meantime, if anything else springs to mind, please get back to me directly.'

They were about to leave when Kerr finally asked a question of his own.

'When did you last see Mr Harvey yourselves?'

'One evening early last week. Tuesday possibly. He was getting into his car just as I got home.'

'Mrs Ahmed?'

'I'm sorry, I can't remember. Not for weeks.'

Ahmed picked up his phone and his case, looked ready to escape. His wife returned her attention to the baby. Jacobson thanked them again and then he and Kerr let themselves out.

Man, woman, child. A simple thing, a sum of three parts. Kerr had never got past two,

Jacobson had fallen from three to one. They headed in silence for the ground floor.

DCs Barber and Hume were covering the top three floors, DCs Williams and Smith took the lower levels. Jacobson and Kerr were making one more housecall themselves before leaving the immediate door-to-door inquiries to the others.

Many of the flats would be empty during the day in any case and their occupants would have to be quizzed in the evening. Some of the flats – like Harvey's – were mortgaged but a property company rented out the lion's share on short lets. Career-driven professionals passing through the area, well-heeled students, couples saving for a house elsewhere; an anonymous anti-community where few could be relied on to know much about their neighbours. Harvey had lived at the very end of the first floor corridor and they'd found out that the flat next door had been unoccupied for three months. There was an outside chance that they might have to trace its most recent inhabitants and interview them. The one facing was occupied on paper but had been empty in response to the doorbell. It couldn't wait till evening: the occupant would need to be tracked down and seen at work if necessary.

Two floors below the Ahmeds and therefore directly under Harvey's terminally stained carpet, the list of residents suggested that at least Mr J. Butler, retired, should still be at home.

Jacobson had to ring the bell three times before the latch-chained door opened a few, cautious inches. Unshaven, Joe Butler stuck a cigarette in his mouth and coughed and farted simultaneously. Jacobson had to hand over his ID for inspection before the old man was prepared to let them in. Where the Ahmed's flat was modern, clean, comfortable, Butler showed them into clutter, dust and neglect.

'There's been no sound all week. I thought he must be off on his jaunts again.'

Kerr was the questioner this time.

'Jaunts, Mr Butler?'

'Jaunts, holidays. He was a professor or something. Off half the year. Me, I was with the gas board forty-three years – week in and week bloody out for most of 'em. I moved here for the wife, to be all on the ground floor, see? With her chest and all. Now she's gone and I'm stuck here. My son phones once a month but he's in Canada.'

The old man's words were drowned by a sudden coughing fit. When it subsided, Kerr brought him back to the point.

'So you knew Roger Harvey then?'

'He called in once in a while right enough. He was interested in the thirties. I was in the CP till the Hitler-Stalin pact, see?'

Kerr nodded, wondering if he'd need to explain the initials to Jacobson afterwards.

'He sent some of his students round once. Oral

17

history project they called it. Young girls too they were.'

'When did you last see him?'

'It must have been three or four weeks ago. He called in one night with a couple of cans of beer. He seemed cheery enough too. I recall him saying that we deserved credit for trying, referring to the old days. You see he was quiet enough, not like some of 'em, but in a block like this you always hear some signs of life if there's somebody in above you.'

Butler paused, lowered his voice as if their talk might have eavesdroppers.

'Especially if they're entertaining a lady friend.'

It was difficult to tell from his rasping voice whether he was disapproving or envious.

'How often—'

'Often enough. Not quite so much in the last couple of months maybe – but I'd say he never went short anyway.'

'But not this week?'

'Last Thursday, I'd say she was last here. 'Course it might not have been the same one each time, eh?'

Jacobson winked conspiratorially at Butler. He wondered what it would be like to be an old man listening in on someone else's pleasure. Kerr put another question.

'Did you ever meet any of his visitors then? Male or female? Did he ever mention any names to you?'

'No. I can't help you there, son. We only talked about the old CP days really. He never gave away very much about himself.'

The ex-gas board ex-communist was seated in front of an old-fashioned writing bureau. The hinged drawer was down revealing an untidy horde of old letters, photograph albums and loose photographs. Jacobson sat close by on an old leather couch and Kerr leant forward from a matching, uncomfortable chair. He hesitated before he put the leading question.

'Were you at home on Sunday night, Mr Butler?'

'No, I certainly wasn't! Not on Remembrance Sunday.'

The old man's eyes seemed almost fierce with sudden pride.

'I'll be at the Cenotaph while my legs can still carry me. The North African campaign was my war – some of the finest lads as ever lived never came back. Anti-fascists. We were going to build the promised land when we got back here. The dreams of youth, see? Every year I'm there. We hold our own do on the Saturday evening. No King and Country stuff either! I stop with an old lad in Lambeth, he was my sergeant then. Eighty-six and still going strong, his wife too.'

Butler halted again, his thoughts rapidly returning to the place where they evidently spent most of their time.

'Anyway, I went down Friday night, got back

Monday lunchtime, see?'

'I see, Mr Butler. Well we probably don't need to disturb you any longer.'

As he stood up, Kerr couldn't help but glance at the bundles of photographs even though he knew where his action would lead. Butler tapped the nearest pile with swollen, arthritic fingers.

'Rambling on the Yorkshire Dales these ones are. The summer of thirty-six. She was a bonny woman in her day.'

'How long since—'

'Last August. We were in Margate for a few days. She always loved the English seaside, wouldn't hear talk of Spain or any of that.'

Neither of them could think of anything that seemed remotely worth saying in reply. The old man had to come to the rescue himself.

'Anyhow, you'd best be getting on. You'll not catch the bugger nattering to me all day.'

Jacobson after Kerr, they shook his hand, left him to his photographs, his battles lost and won.

'The super's arrangement, first thing. Complete forensic examination of the vehicle. If the assailant knew Harvey then there could be evidence – might've given his murderer a lift back from the pub, whatever. How's it going, son?'

'It's definitely the deep end, Sergeant.'

Sergeant Ince, uniformed liaison officer for the inquiry, and young PC Ogden, freshly graduated from Hendon, watched the victim's car being loaded on to the recovery vehicle.

'The best way, believe me.'

The wind, which had died down briefly, got up strongly again. Ogden glanced round in the opposite direction. The flats and their car park were at the very edge of the estate. The start of a bridleway ran down behind the car park and out into a small wood. Beyond the right of way was farmland which had been set aside: heaven-sent terrain in which to conceal a murder weapon or bloody clothing.

As soon as the full complement arrived, one body of uniformed officers would search the fields while another would extend the door-to-door work to the semis. For now, CID would hog the probably more fruitful inquiries in the block itself.

The recovery vehicle rattled away and they were joined by Jacobson and Kerr.

'We're calling in at the university next, Sergeant. Can you get somebody to drive the DS's car back to the Divi before lunchtime?'

'No problem at all, sir.'

Ince went quiet for a moment and Jacobson saw what was coming.

'Do we know yet whether we'll be setting up a forward station out here? Only—'

'Ince, old son, it's not justified. Anybody who's looking to play cards and clock up overtime better do it on some other bastard's expense sheet. You'll need a twenty-four watch for the time being though – maintain the security of the place, but that can be a one-man-per-shift duty. We can do everything else from the incident room.'

Sergeant Ince knew an incorruptible brick wall when he saw one. Still – as he said to Ogden after they'd gone – there'd been no harm in trying.

Jacobson and Kerr reviewed the case on their way across town. Although the police surgeon had pronounced Harvey dead, the initial forensic tests would be taken care of by late afternoon and the autopsy would be completed before then, there was still the issue of formal identification outstanding. Harvey was unmarried, the only son of deceased parents and his associates were still unknown. While Ahmed or Butler could do the job at a pinch, they decided to ask someone from the university to do the honours. But it wasn't the procedural details which were niggling Jacobson: ever since Merchant had refined and expanded Robinson's 'a couple of days anyway' into an estimate of 'three or more likely four days', he'd known that – overriding everything else – his main obstacle was the clock.

Harvey had probably been killed in the early hours of Monday morning and now it was Thursday. Murders unsolved in the first twenty-four hours are sometimes never solved; in the Harvey case somewhere in excess of ninety-six hours had probably slipped by. He gave the steering wheel a futile punch with his left fist.

'Christ, Ian, there's going to be more than bloody flies buzzing round this one.'

Maybe the Ahmeds had overheard a murder as well as an argument. Maybe. Maybe there was a distraught, unbalanced soul out there somewhere – sitting patiently for the police to get to them, waiting penitently for the balm of confession. Maybe. Maybe instead there was a killer determined to get away, who'd already gained the time to hide, conceal, construct an alibi:

'The time, Ian, old son, to get out the effing country.'

Professor Merchant closed the door and waited until Robinson's footsteps faded down the corridor. Robinson had been understandably keyed-up for the autopsy of his first murder victim. Merchant's advice had hardly been original or surprising – just forget the presence of the video camera, explain each stage in plain English wherever possible, don't dwell on how the corpse got to be there, let the routine, the procedures, take over and carry him through it. Nevertheless it had been effective: Robinson had left Merchant's office almost convinced he'd be able to do it.

Merchant had never forgotten his own first time. In those less censorious days, his professor had poured him a generous tot of whisky beforehand. By God, he'd needed it. All the training in the world, he'd realised, couldn't prepare you for your first close-up encounter with the damage one human being was capable of deliberately inflicting on another. The memory of it could still make him flinch.

He picked up his phone and dialled seven for an outside line. His fingers conjured up a number from memory but instead of the expected ringing tone, a grating, electronically generated voice informed him he had dialled incorrectly. He rummaged in his desk for an address book, flicked through the pages and tried again. This time the number rang.

It rang fourteen times before someone relented and answered his call.

Crowby University. Harvey's place of work was a landscape of grey concrete and sparse green shrubbery which even in summer would be scarcely more colourful than it was now. The students too were mostly dressed in the drab colours of winter as they hurried from building to building in the harshening wind.

A young man wearing the uniform of CrowbyGuard Security didn't seem particularly pleased to see them, didn't bother to ask their business as they entered the administration building. Croucher, the vice chancellor, appeared in person to greet them and brought them, via a staircase marked 'staff only', to his own suite of offices. Independently of each other, Kerr and

Jacobson considered mentioning the vetting of private security firms, the form of the junior villain downstairs. Something about the impeccably polite manner of their guide encouraged both of them towards the same, instinctive conclusion: it's not my problem, mate, let him work it out for himself when the photocopiers and the computer chips go walking.

A secretary, who'd been watering an overgrown cheeseplant in the outer office, brought in a tray of tea and coffee. On the wall behind Croucher's expansive desk, a large Paolozzi depicted the colourful and convincingly intricate mechanisms of an entirely imaginary machine. Kerr studied it in detail while Croucher intoned stock condolences. Why, he wondered, did members of the public so often react as if it was the police themselves who'd been suddenly bereaved?

Dr Harvey, Croucher insisted on telling them, had been a very talented scholar indeed. He'd been popular amongst the students, respected by his colleagues. It was dreadful news, terrible news. He couldn't imagine why anyone would want to do such a thing. Jacobson interrupted him in mid-cliché.

'Can you tell us, sir, why no one seems to have noticed his absence from the university all week?'

Croucher eyed Jacobson with all the disdain available to a member of the Reform Club and of government committees too numerous to mention. His well-modulated voice only barely smoothed his annoyance at being cut short.

'Dr Harvey was on a year's sabbatical leave. He would have been around the university on an informal basis and I believe he was maintaining his input into several course development teams but there would be absolutely no reason to think anything other than that he was carrying on his research at home.'

Kerr followed the frosty exchange, glad that he'd taken a back seat for the interview. It was perfectly obvious that Croucher knew precisely nothing about Harvey on a personal basis, probably wouldn't have recognised him in the corridor. They may have had a murder to investigate but it was all too clear that the university's senior executive only wanted to tick the box marked no bad publicity. While Jacobson ploughed on, Kerr daydreamed himself dead, shot up by a deranged gunman or his head kicked in by tearaways on crack. The chief constable would have to substitute the brave officer for the talented scholar but otherwise he'd be able to borrow large chunks of Croucher's testimonial verbatim if the need arose. He listened inattentively as the predictable answers were given, the obvious arrangements made. They ought to meet Dr Lombard next, '– excellent chap, he'll be able to fill in more of the, ah, personal detail. Probably the best man to handle the identification too.'

It struck Kerr that the functions of the top cop and the vice chancellor were virtually identical. Neither did any real work, both spent most of their time papering over the cracks. It didn't surprise him in the least when, just as they were leaving, Croucher grew suddenly effusive about the university's good relations with the force in general – and over his recent convivial dinner in the company of the chief constable in particular. The Boss Class, as his father had always argued, liked to stick together.

Lombard, the Dean of Humanities, was a large man with a beard. He was wearing an ill-fitting yellow shirt and an ill-chosen tie which depicted the Statue of Liberty in Day-Glo reds and blues. By contrast, his face, as far as it was visible, was white as a sheet. He apologised needlessly for the state of his office, the sprawl of papers on his desk.

'I've . . . I've been on a course for the last three days – Managing Change in Education.'

Jacobson nodded patiently, repeated his question. In a murder case, he reminded himself, there was no wholly extraneous information.

'Y-yes of course I'll help with the identification. I just can't believe what you're telling me. He was sitting right where you are just last week, as large as life.'

'What day would that have been?'

'W-Wednesday, Wednesday. He'd been

27

working in the library and called in for a chat. We're planning some changes to the teaching programme in the new term and I wanted to keep him in touch.'

Lombard fingered his clumsily knotted tie as he answered Jacobson's questions. No, Roger Harvey hadn't appeared anxious or worried. On the contrary, he seemed to be making the most of his year off, at least as far as his research was concerned.

'The rumour was that he'd got one of the big publishers interested in terms of a coffee table book, maybe even a tie-in to a tv documentary.'

'What exactly was Dr Harvey's field then?'

'He's – he was – a specialist in the history of Europe between the wars. He did his doctoral work on the Spanish Civil War and the International Brigades. More recently, he'd been working on Nazi Germany.'

'And he could do that from here in Crowby?'

'Certainly – at the writing-up stage anyway. He'd already been out to Munich in the spring to check the archive material he needed.'

Lombard's nervous fingers switched their jumpy attention from his tie to his beard. Jacobson asked him if he could shed any light on Harvey's personal life.

'Not a great deal. I gather he always had some girlfriend or other on the go but I never met any of them. He never attended official university functions if he could help it, never stayed long if he couldn't. To be honest, I think he saw himself as only passing through Crowby on his way to somewhere better – as soon as he'd got enough publications under his belt, of course. The man you really need to speak to is John Kent, our head of history. He and his wife were both close to Dr Harvey – I believe they first met when they were all students together.'

'Perhaps he could identify the body then, Dr Lombard, spare you—'

'No, Inspector, really, I feel steadier now. It's just not what you expect to happen to someone you actually know. Anyway, John was with me when the vice chancellor phoned through. At my suggestion, he's cancelled his classes and gone home to break the news to his wife.'

Chapter Two

Kerr's lunch was a triangular pack of limp cheese sandwiches which he'd bought in a petrol station and eaten in a lay-by. Ten minutes later, eight miles from Crowby's urban sprawl, he turned his car into the rural congestion of Wynarth's market square. He made it past the Bank House and the Viceroy Tandoori only to find the road ahead blocked by a green delivery lorry which was backing slowly and gingerly into the narrow alley at the side of Humphrey's Wine Bar. There seemed to be unloading and unpacking underway in every direction, even something large and bulky being awkwardly manoeuvred through the doors of the Flotation Centre.

As soon as the van cleared his path, he edged out of the square on the north side towards the rows of nineteenth-century villas and terraces. Wynarth's geography was as stratified as an army barracks. The leafy lanes on the perimeter brought you to the secluded driveways and substantial properties of the seriously wealthy but the centre was under occupation by middle-class, middle-income newcomers. There were therapists here, talks about Tantric Buddhism, Greenpeace meetings. Kerr reckoned he knew the pattern of streets well enough yet he drove past Balance Wholefoods twice – the Looking East Gallery three times – and in the end had to ask directions from a young woman who was coming out of the bookshop before he found his way.

When he finally got to the Kents' place, he drew up a few doors further down the street. It was an old instinct from his patrol car days: never announce your presence unnecessarily.

John Kent showed Kerr through the hall to the kitchen where Annie Kent was on gin and cigarettes at the round pine table. At first glance, the husband seemed more composed than the wife but there was a glass of Bell's in his hand and a rheumy look in his eyes behind his glasses.

There are three ways long-standing couples age: at the same rate, woman first/man second or man first/woman second. The Kents were firmly in the third category. A short, balding man running to paunch and a tall, pre-Raphaelite beauty.

Kerr drank in her body as she struggled with the effort of kettle, milk, teabag. Long, shapely legs emphasised by tight black jeans, long black curls cascading over her shoulders, the curve of full breasts undisguised by a pink silk blouse. He did the arithmetic. Both Kents were in their early forties: take ten years off her, add them to him and you arrived at the sum of how they actually looked.

'Why don't you just sit down, Annie? Let me do it.'

Careful with his whisky, Kent took the shaking kettle from his wife's hands, watched her sit down.

'I understand you had known Mr eh, Dr Harvey for a long time.'

The stated question was for no one in particular. Kerr waited for one of them to pick it up. Kent placed an Oxfam mug in front of him. Central America is Dying for Change.

'Yes. Getting on for fifteen years. Annie and I were postgraduates, living together on limited cash. We cleared out a spare room and sub-let it. We had a virtual queue of people round but Roger got both our votes. He seemed so young and shy in those days. I think he brought out Annie's maternal instincts.'

Instincts that must have since gone unsatisfied: like his own house, the Kents' domestic interior lacked any sign of babies, children or adolescents. Mrs Kent drew on her cigarette, spoke for the first time.

'He was only in his second year, I think. Some girl had thrown him over. He was on the verge of giving up his course. John took him down the pub, talked him out of it.'

The hint of a smile crossed her face at the memory. Kent stood behind his wife, gently stroking her hair, the back of her neck. It evidently took her an effort of will to draw herself back to the present.

'We've been friends ever since. John told him about the job at Crowby before it was advertised. We were both delighted when he got it.'

'Which was when?'

'It must have been about seven years ago, wasn't it John?'

'Eight I would have said. He did a spell in the north-east, some technical college or other, while he finished off his doctorate. Crowby was his first real appointment.'

Kerr sipped at the tea, felt the Kents' collective gaze. He was an intruder into private mourning – it was part of what he was paid for.

'We don't think there was an obvious criminal motive for the murder, which suggests that the actual motive may have been personal in some way. Can you think of anybody, any reason?'

'It's really too bizarre. If they don't like you in our work, they don't promote you or they rubbish your views in an article. They don't murder you. Perhaps you're suggesting a student did it over low marks or a lost essay?'

'The fact is somebody *did* murder him, Mr Kent – sorry – Dr Kent.'

'Call me John for Christ's sake. Look, I'm

sorry too, I realise you've got a job to do but Annie and I – we've thought of nothing else for an hour. We can't imagine who on earth would have a reason.'

'I appreciate this isn't easy, believe me. We've been told Dr Harvey had a girlfriend. Do either of you know her?'

Mrs Kent started to speak but her husband cut across her with a laugh which sounded more like a snort.

'Roger and his girlfriends! He seemed to change them more often than most men change their underpants.'

He took a large hit of whisky and his wife tried again.

'John is inclined to exaggerate sometimes, Sergeant. Roger was never married – obviously he had a number of relationships over the years.'

'Including recently then?'

'The most recent was Melissa. Melissa Woolstone – she was a librarian at the university. She left Crowby back in April and went off to work in New Zealand of all places. It must've been around the time that Roger was in Munich. That's right, isn't it, John?'

Kent nodded his agreement, put down his empty whisky glass.

'I shouldn't think Roger was too upset. He certainly wasn't planning to settle down with a wife and a regular order for the *Radio Times*; might've got in the way of his career for one thing.'

Annie Kent brushed a black ringlet from her forehead.

'But, as I've said, he wasn't always like that. Maybe it was because after that girl—'

'Oh yes, Alison. There's a name that takes you back. Do you know I think that's about the only time I ever saw Roger close to tears.'

Kent stroked his wife's hair again and this time both of them seemed to fall into a silent reverie.

Kerr had only lasted five months at university himself. He'd packed it in halfway through the first year, bored by the work and sickened by the relentless pretentiousness of his fellow students. While he could probably have looked into Annie's misty eyes all afternoon in their own right, the Kents' mutual nostalgia for their long-gone student days was starting to irritate him.

'So – anyway – Dr Harvey took his work seriously?'

Kent poured himself out another generous measure and finally sat down to join them at the table.

'A couple of articles every year was his absolute minimum. Not to mention two well-received books and a third on the way.'

'Dr Lombard said something about him not staying put in Crowby.'

Kent's face was a small round moon with two smaller moons, the oval lenses of his glasses, in parallel orbit around it. He reminded Kerr of a sad-looking owl. He gave another snorting laugh before he answered.

'Our bearded leader is entirely correct for once. Roger definitely had big league aspirations. Oxbridge, Harvard, something like that.'

Kerr took another sip of tea and fixed the important details in his mind. According to his neighbour, Joe Butler, there had been a woman in Harvey's flat as recently as last Thursday yet the Kents were saying his girlfriend had left town in April. He wondered how well they really knew their old friend after all.

'When did you last see or hear from Dr Harvey?'

'It was last Thursday, Sergeant. John and Roger played squash and then I cooked them dinner.'

'Yes, a regular fixture for us most weeks. It's the only exertion I take which is why Roger never loses – never lost – a game. Usually the three of us would go round to the Wynarth Arms afterwards. There's a band there we like on Thursdays. They play all the old rhythm and blues stuff.'

Kerr knew the pub, had heard the band himself a couple of times. According to Cathy, the bass player had gigged with the late, great Steve Marriott for a while. He watched Annie Kent's elegant, awkward fingers light up another cigarette and decided it wasn't the right moment to be passing on rock trivia.

'And you went there last Thursday?'

'We did but Roger didn't. He ate with us but then he said he was tired, that he wanted an early night for a change.'

'Annie's right. He must have left here about a quarter to ten.'

No matter how close someone was to you, Kerr thought, you never knew everything about another person. You never knew for instance when the last time you'd see them alive might be.

'So you didn't see him over the weekend?'

Kent had emptied his glass again, was filling it up again. He looked even older and wearier than the fifty he could normally pass for.

'No, we were on our narrowboat. Cut across from Castlefoot Lock and had a look at the Grand Union Canal. We left on Friday and drove back after breakfast on Monday morning. I've no classes till Monday afternoon this term so we've been taking full advantage of the weekends to get away.'

Lombard had identified the body of Roger Harvey with an outward show of calm. Maybe he'd finally got a grip on his nerves or maybe, as was common, they'd mount a counter attack later. He'd still been wearing his garish tie. At least, Jacobson thought, he hadn't puked up over truth, justice and the American way.

After Lombard had gone, Jacobson mingled with the other lucky contestants who were officially obliged to attend the performance of the autopsy. He talked football with Robinson, concealing his personal indifference for the game and for sport in general: the young man was evidently in need of some distraction from the task ahead. Everybody was as ready as they were ever going to be but predictably there was no sign yet of Merchant. There were after all a full three minutes left before the appointed time of two o'clock. Merchant had never been known to be late but somehow it was more annoying – almost infuriating – that he would show up exactly and precisely on time.

Jacobson just wanted to get the ugly business over with, to get back on with the investigation. There wasn't much chance of instant enlightenment in the mortuary in any case. It would take twenty-four hours to turn round the detailed analysis of body samples and, for all the advances in pathology, it was still usually only a range of possibilities rather than a precise point which could be plotted for the time of death.

He glanced warily at the corpse laid out in readiness on the operating table. Stomach content was crucial in narrowing the band of possible times. Perhaps they'd strike lucky. Harvey might have stuffed himself with a couple of pork pies and a mega-burger with giant fries before meeting his demise. Then again, in these health-conscious times, he might just as easily turn out to have been a fanatical vegetarian.

*

Barber and Hume. Williams and Smith. Two pairs of detective constables. Three floors of the crime scene building each. Result: zero. As expected, the majority of the flat dwellers had either been out or had pretended to be out. Less than one in four had answered their doors and those had less than nothing to say. They'd never heard of Roger Harvey, didn't recognise his photo. Listen, mate, they didn't know who lived next door, never mind three floors down.

Kerr told them to take a break. Driving back, he'd noticed a Lite Bite amongst the bleakly tidy row of shops in the middle of the estate. They could grab a cuppa, even risk a sausage roll if they felt like living dangerously. The DCs had been working their way steadily upwards. Reversing the process for no particular reason, Kerr took the stairs to the top floor. As he stepped into the corridor, a thundering bass riff ear-butted him with the force of an unanticipated punch in the guts. Grimacing, he made straight for the source. At least *somebody* was definitely in, at least he could show them how a volume control worked.

The door of the flat in question had been recently painted in the deepest black. The list of residents showed it as the address of Ms J. Wells. It took a sustained combination of bell ringing, letterbox rattling and finally a hefty kick before some shuffling could be detected from inside. The door opened slightly on a chain, pushing the noise beyond the pain threshold.

'Fuck off! We'll play it as loud as we like.'

The voice was young, female, screechy. Kerr shoved his warrant card through the gap to immediate effect.

'Turn it down, Brian. It's police.'

A girl about twenty with long black hair, flashing black eyes and a white face gashed by black lipstick undid the chain and drew the door back. She showed him into a black interior where thick black curtains kept the daylight at bay. Brian, a broad, sturdy youth, whose clothes betrayed a similarly restricted interest in colour, turned the hi-fi down with a show of nonchalance. A second unnamed youth, whose T-shirt conceded a jagged strip of red across the chest, continued to strum an unplugged electric guitar.

Kerr tried out an appropriate-sounding lie.

'My brother's into thrash metal but he does sometimes draw the curtains.'

The girl sat down next to Brian and the unnamed youth put the guitar down. Brian spoke.

'Look if it's that old bag again, we agreed we'd only have the volume up in the afternoons. Live and let live.'

'I'm pleased to hear it but that's not why I'm here.'

He told them why. The youths looked less pleased with themselves, the girl looked anxious.

'You mean Dr Harvey from the university?'

'I'm afraid so. You knew him then?'

'I did a history course in my first year. He was my tutor in the summer term.'

'So you're all students?'

The unnamed youth looked up.

'Jane is, part of the time anyway. Otherwise her parents wouldn't pay the rent on this place.'

'But mainly I'm with the band.'

'Jane on bass and vocals, Brian on drums, I'm Phil, the guitarmeister.'

Kerr looked round the room, studied the contents. Now that his eyes had adjusted to the gloom, he could take in a large poster on the far wall. It showed the girl and the two young men posed moodily in an alleyway surrounded by garbage and graffiti. Above their heads, in intended contrast, a ruined castle perched on craggy rocks and a bird with outspread wings was silhouetted against a gibbous moon. At the bottom of the poster he read the legend '*CROWBLACK* – the *GOTH*ic revival!'

Brian finally switched the hi-fi off completely while Phil drew back the curtains slightly. In the fields beyond, the police search was underway.

'Fuck! We saw him on Sunday, didn't we?'

He looked at the other two as he sat back down. Brian spoke again.

'Phil's right. Over the Bison's. The Bison's Head. Not much of a boozer but it's the nearest we've got to one, living out here. We usually end up there on a Sunday afternoon sooner or later. Anyway Harvey was at the bar when we got

41

there . . . along with his creepy neighbour.'

Kerr asked him exactly which neighbour he meant.

'The one in the flat opposite Harvey's gaff. I don't know his name. Leching bastard though. Can't keep his eyes off Jane, any time he sees her.'

Kerr circled the name Mitchell in the list of residents. The property company had been slow to get their act together but finally they'd checked their tenancy references and had come up with a workplace address for Harvey's nearest neighbour. Jacobson should have got there by now, was probably already talking to him.

Jane pulled Brian's arm around her as if she felt suddenly cold. Her accent was an odd mixture: posh playing at estuary.

'They were both dressed as if they'd been jogging. I've seen them occasionally before, out running on the bridleway.'

'What time on Sunday would this have been?'

Phil finally lit up the roll-up he'd spent the last minute studiously manufacturing.

'Must've been around three. I'd been over in Wynarth to see a guy about an amp and Jane and Brian had – well, they'd only just got up.'

Kerr looked for the hint of a blush under the surface of the girl's china-white makeup but didn't find it. He asked if any of them had spoken to either Harvey or his neighbour.

'Nah. They left soon after we got there. Harvey nodded across at Jane as they were leaving and the other guy's eyes were on stilts as usual. I remember Brian saying afterwards that he would have to have a word with the sad old case one of these days.'

'Too right mate. It's Jane that keeps saying don't worry about it, don't pay him any attention.'

The drummer's arm had still been draped around the girl's shoulders but now she disentangled herself from his protection.

'Listen to Mr Macho! I know you can look after yourself, Brian, you don't have to prove it all the time. Anyway, there's something about that geezer – it's not just his size. I don't know what it is really. I just wouldn't want to get on the wrong side of him, that's all.'

'And you didn't see Roger Harvey or this neighbour of his later in the day?'

Phil balanced his roll-up on the side of a black ashtray.

'No again. We came back here after a couple of drinks and rested up for an hour or so. Then we had to drive over to Leicester for a gig. Brian's brother's got a place over there so we had a bit of a session after the gig. We didn't drive back till Monday morning.'

Jacobson took the lift to the seventeenth floor of Pelican House and entered the spacious, air-conditioned office of Tony Davies. The nameplate on the door had announced him as Senior Project

Manager, Eschaton Systems. Through the wall-sized, hermetically sealed window, he could see the lights of Crowby holding out against the darkening afternoon. A real-life bird – some kind of hawk – hovered a few yards from the window for a moment then was gone in flight. Davies identified it as a kestrel.

'We often see them at this level. I suppose it's because we're bordering on the countryside out here. Gives you a bit of a trapped feeling, really, watching them soar past a window you can't even open.'

Jacobson didn't have the time to spare immediately for a discussion about the meaning of life.

'I know what you mean, but about Mr Mitchell—'

'Yes, of course. My apologies. The thing is we'd like to know where David Mitchell is too.'

Davies paused and picked up a bundle of papers from his desk.

'He was supposed to be on a three-day course in Birmingham. When he didn't come here as he should have done today my people checked with the organisers.

'Apparently he phoned them with some excuse on Monday morning and never showed there at all. Also, as you already know, he doesn't seem to be at his flat. We've been trying his permanent address all day with no response.'

'His permanent address?'

'Mitchell is a contract programmer, a specialist

in expert systems and neural networks. We had to bring him in to help with a priority project. We prefer to use full-time permanent staff but sometimes situations develop and there's no other option. We hired Mitchell in August. He seemed to know his stuff – that's why we were prepared to send him to Birmingham. The course would really have been more use to him for future contracts than for what he was doing for us. Sort of a bonus for his hard work.'

'And no one's heard from him all week?'

'We all work flexi-time here. According to the printout, he keyed in about nine thirty on Sunday morning and keyed back out at one fifteen pm. He'd been in for six hours on Saturday as well. Overtime. Like I say he's been a hard worker – but he hasn't been in the building since then.'

Davies passed the bundle of papers over to Jacobson.

'A photocopy of his personnel file. His home address, all the details are there. The murder was on the news at lunchtime. I knew the address was familiar but I didn't make the connection until you phoned. Do you think he's got something to do with it?'

'It's usually best not to speculate in advance, Mr Davies, but we obviously want to find Mr Mitchell fast. It might be best if you said nothing to your other staff in the meantime.'

He helped himself to Davies' phone.

'That's right. David Mitchell – and it's a Coventry address.'

At ten minutes to five, Jacobson gathered the team in the incident room, now fully set up, for his second briefing of the day. He was holding a newly faxed copy of Robinson's autopsy report in one hand and the inevitable B and H in the other.

'Anyone with the stomach for it who thinks it might help can catch the video after they've studied the report. Operationally, David Mitchell is obviously our man of the moment. It's entirely possible that his disappearance is just pure coincidence, of course. But even if it isn't, we've still got a case to build. We've no idea for instance who the woman was that the Ahmeds say they overheard or what the hell Mitchell's – or anybody else's – motive might have been. Bear in mind too that the autopsy findings are still subject to the final lab reports. The time frame's not exactly narrow either: after midnight but before three am. The proverbial blunt instrument was brass and heavy but as you know there's been no joy so far in the search for the weapon. The first blow looks to have been struck from behind, probably taking the victim by surprise. He would have been unconscious after the second or third blow. The culprit just went on hitting and hitting.'

Kerr had taken a back seat for the briefing again. He stopped listening to Jacobson's recap and recalled instead his earlier comments regarding buzzing flies and the time-gap since the murder.

If he *had* done it, Mitchell could have flown round the world twice in the interim.

The Brewer's Rest matched its uninspired name to an uninspired interior. Mock oak beams, mock fire, mock food. Jacobson frequented it solely on account of its nearness to the Divisional building, a proximity which also extended to the newest of Crowby's three shopping malls and to the national headquarters of a large insurance company. On Thursday nights, this made for crowds and special presentations. Later, after Happy Hour, it would be Coco-Rico Nite: the bar staff were already assembling instant palm trees and balancing precariously on tables to hang lines of red, green and silver decorations from the plastic oak beams.

Jacobson downed the first half of his pint in one and found himself a secluded corner. He didn't really like drinking on his own, not in public anyway. But one by one the team had evaded his invitation, paraded their excuses. He supposed he didn't blame them. There were long hours ahead for all of them, trying to claw back lost time. The early evening break was precious, not to be frittered away if you had any kind of a personal life to fit in between shifts. Everybody it seemed had somewhere more important to be except for himself.

He watched the place continuing to fill up. If he wanted a refill he'd need to work his way through a three-deep crowd at the bar. He wondered where Janice was, what she was doing. Not in general but right now, that very moment. It would be four and a half years soon, as long ago as the Crawler investigation. 'I expect it'll be some days before you notice I've gone and some days before you find this note.' Not true! He'd noticed long before. The new hair-dos, the evening classes which became more and more frequent, the phone-calls which ended just as he came through the door. Two decades they'd spent together! Of course he was going to say something, sort it out, make things right. If only she could have waited until after the case. To leave him for someone like Mackeson as well: a property speculator, only just this side of the law. It had felt like a rejection of his total existence, of his work and his values as well as of himself. She'd danced on their marriage as if it had been the tomb of a fallen enemy.

Two young women sat down at the next table. He had already classified them as secretaries before it occurred to him how hopelessly out of date so many of his stock responses had become. They were just as likely to be doctors or solicitors or civil engineers. The nearest one took off her jacket. She wore a long, loose-fitting skirt but her breasts were crammed in against a tight blue T-shirt which plunged at the neckline and bulged at the nipples. Jacobson's glance became a stare.

He drained his glass and stood up to leave, abandoning his idea of a second pint and a whisky chaser. It wasn't bad enough that his wife had left him or that he was drinking and smoking himself towards an early grave: now he'd become a dirty old man into the bargain.

Cathy was poring over sales figures in the front room when Kerr got back. The wreckage from the night before remained exactly where it had been.

'Brought work home again?'

He'd meant it as a neutral, inconsequential remark but she took it as the bell for seconds out, round two.

'It gives me something to do while you're out planting evidence and harassing the public.'

The look on her face confirmed that it was too soon for negotiations, too early for a cessation of hostilities.

'You could at least try some original sarcasm once in a while. You know murder inquiries are top priority. I won't be back on normal shifts till I'm off the team and the case is solved. I don't suppose there's any—'

'In the kitchen. It's ready. Just stick it in the microwave for five minutes.'

He banged the door behind him on his way through. What she'd meant by ready was that she'd taken the packet out of the freezer and stuck it on the table. Rogan Josh, the authentic Indian taste in minutes. According to the labelling, it was a full and delicious serving for one. He cut himself a thick slice of bread while it cooked just in case.

He ate without enthusiasm, washing his food down with nothing stronger than Perrier. The kitchen was quiet except for the steady ticking of the clock and the cat purring sleepily, unconcernedly, on the windowsill. He decided to catch up with the latest news on the local BBC station. Predictably, the Harvey case was the lead story. Economic calamities and foreign massacres were no match for foul play in your own backyard as far as the great British public was concerned. Disappointingly, no doubt, the report was sparse on gruesome detail.

'Local police are investigating the death of a local university lecturer whose body was discovered earlier today although the murder is believed to have taken place in the early hours of Monday morning—'

Kerr pushed his plate to one side and picked up an apple.

'The inquiry is being headed by Chief Inspector Jacobson who was commended four years ago for the successful arrest and conviction of the multiple rapist dubbed by the press as the Crowby Crawler.'

Commended and then passed over to be

precise. Jacobson had made himself too useful as a workhorse, had spent too little time on the politics of the force, to have a chance of promotion upstairs. Kerr still felt guilty for turning down his invitation to the pub even though he'd done so in good faith, intending to make up with Cathy.

He bit hopefully into the apple but it turned out to be as blandly tasteless as the phoney curry. The details of the argument had stayed fuzzy but he realised now that he'd been carrying the hurt around with him all day. Their childlessness had been her big issue as usual. The emptiness which could never be breached, the gap which could never be filled. It was as if she needed one, single demon to blame for everything else. Maybe it was easier to deal with that way, maybe he should try it himself.

He switched the radio off, noticed the clock again.

The worst thing was how he'd started to feel about the job. Only another ten minutes and he could escape back to the investigation.

Chapter Three

The River Crow was wide and deep running. At this point, a mile and a half from the centre of town, it flowed close to a tree-lined park, the legacy of a civic-minded Victorian magnate. The park was widely favoured for family strolls in summer and equally widely looked on as dangerous after dark: two sides of the same, ambiguous, urban coin.

The river and the park were heavily featured in Crowby's latest promotional literature. On shiny covers, hang-gliders soared over water and trees in bright July sunshine, trailing the slogan, 'Fly High in Crowby!' In the Crowby Riverside Hotel, a pile of the new pamphlets had been stacked on the reception desk next to the brochures for the Riverside Health Club and Sauna.

The receptionist was tired out and not bothering to hide it, despite all the corporate training to the contrary which she'd been compelled to receive. Her fingers traced a weary line across a street plan as she tried to give directions to a Japanese executive whose English was untypically bad. Another time, Professor Merchant might have grabbed the opportunity to demonstrate his multi-lingual capacities but, under the circumstances, he walked briskly past and made straight for the cocktail bar.

Looking around, he saw that his expectations had been correct. The other customers were mainly – and sparsely – transient businessmen and women: Crowby today and gone tomorrow. He took his seat at a dimly lit table and, lifting a glass to his lips, savoured the peaty taste of his favourite Islay malt.

The woman wore leather trousers and her brown hair was spiky short. She glared at him as if her eyes were daggers. He noticed that the lines on her face had grown deeper since he'd last seen her. Up close, her skin, without makeup, was blotchy. Her voice was quiet but mocking.

'Ally Merchant! Always exactly on time, like Mussolini's trains.'

Merchant put down his drink and smiled an unsmiling smile. He'd forgotten how hard she'd been to cope with in the end, how relieved he'd been to unload her on to Roger Harvey.

'Thanks for the whisky. I didn't think you'd remember. Cheers.'

'Cheers yourself, shitbag.'

Merchant persisted in his pre-decided strategy of politeness.

'How's the hostel doing?'

'How do you think? Overloaded and under-funded. We're still turning women away every day, sending them back home for another beating.'

'That's partly why I felt we should meet. I expect the last thing you need is bad publicity.'

She glared at him a second time.

'Bad publicity for the hostel? You are such a hypocrite, Ally. It wouldn't be your own reputation that's worrying you, of course – or certain things you'd prefer your wife not to read about over her muesli?'

Merchant looked anxiously around but no one seemed to be paying them the slightest attention. He knew only too well her propensity for making a scene. He hoped to God she wasn't going to start one right now.

'I almost feel like selling the story to the papers myself, just for the hell of it. "Pathologist's Affair Linked to Murder Hunt." How's it sound to you, Ally?'

Laura Gregory finished off her own whisky in a swift gulp. Merchant estimated from the occasional slur in her speech that she was already carrying more than a few. He didn't answer her and they fell into a mutual silence for several minutes. She lit a cigarette and blew the smoke, which she knew he detested, towards his face. He realised that she was enjoying his having to be there, his having to get in touch with her. There was nothing he could do but submit to his punishment. Finally, she spoke again, touching his forearm lightly across the table.

'Oh, relax, Ally. You and Roger had that in common didn't you? Complete self-centredness: the other kind of violence that men inflict on women. Christ, how do I pick them?'

Merchant hesitated, fingered the edge of a beermat.

'So, we can agree stories then?'

'Well, we can't have the professor in the papers, can we? Although to be honest with you, I can't see what the problem is. Why should the police even be interested?'

Her promised compliance disconcerted him nearly as much as her anger. It crossed his mind uncomfortably that the price of her cooperation might be a resumption of their relationship.

'If they do their job properly with Roger's papers and letters they might get to you. You could even be a suspect if they hear about how you behaved when you split up with him.'

He regretted the euphemism immediately.

'Look, Ally, if you want to cook the books with me then cut out the newspeak. I didn't split up with Roger, Roger ditched me for the library bimbo. Only, unlike yourself – a cad of the old school – he didn't have the good grace to recruit a replacement first.'

Merchant took another sip of whisky and started to wish that she'd got him a double.

'Whatever you say, Laura. Whatever description you wish.'

Kerr was driving back to Roger Harvey's flat, back to the book-crammed rooms and the blood-blackened carpet. He fiddled with the waveband, caught the end of a Bob Marley track. But the station turned out to be German or Dutch and 'Stir It Up' was followed by what sounded like a phone-in programme. He switched back reluctantly to Radio One on FM and turned into the winding street which led to the crime scene.

Seven nights ago, possibly to the minute, Roger Harvey had been driving too – over to the Kents' at Wynarth. The game of squash, the meal in Annie Kent's kitchen and, later, if Joe Butler had been accurate, the rendezvous with an unidentified woman. John Kent had said that he wasn't looking to settle down. According to Dr Lombard, he'd always had some girlfriend or other on the go. Women had slept with him, friends had sought him out, yet Harvey had gone his own way, immersed in his research. Some would have called him self-absorbed, even selfish. But the way Kerr saw it, Harvey had succeeded in living alone without loneliness, free to pay his bills and pursue his interests. He ignored the lift again and took the stairs to the first floor, recognising the envy he felt for what it was. His conscious mind at last grasped a fact which his unconscious had long since digested: he was thinking about leaving Cathy.

Harvey's writing was everywhere in the flat but nearly all of it was impersonal. Lecture notes, notes made in the margins of books and journals, rough drafts of reviews. On the off chance, he booted up Harvey's computer. The file directory fanned down the screen, confirming electronically the impression of a man whose work was central to his existence. As far as Kerr was able to tell, all the files were related in one way or another to Harvey's book on the Third Reich, now never to be completed. He switched the machine off, considered where to look next. Somewhere in the handful of rooms, the dead man had surely left more intimate traces of his life than these.

He let himself get distracted a second time by Harvey's collection of records and cds. Ry Cooder, Van Morrison again, Dylan, Counting Crows, a rare REM bootleg. No doubt Harvey had known as much about police work as Kerr knew about historical research, yet they could have been jukebox brothers if nothing else. Apart from the bootleg, he had most of this stuff at home himself. The only thing he could fault was the presence of several compilations of drum'n'bass or trip-hop or jungle or whatever they were calling dance music this week. Kerr had always felt that it was cheating if the sampler and the drum machine did all the work. Now he wondered if maybe he'd got it wrong after all, had somehow missed the point. Maybe Cathy had been right when she'd claimed, amongst many other complaints, that becoming a copper had made him straight-arsed, narrow-minded, conservative.

Eventually he came to the drawer in the kitchen intended for cutlery but which Harvey, it seemed, had used for another purpose. His passport was there and so was his birth certificate, medical card, insurance policy documents, several unopened bank statements and a letter, also unopened, from the Inland Revenue. Finally, next to an out of date programme for the Crowby Film Theatre, he found a bundle of what looked like private letters held together by a broad elastic band and an ageing address book with a battered, brown leather cover.

Kerr glanced through the well-worn pages. They were creased, coffee-stained, occasionally torn. Under the name 'Mitchell', two phone numbers were listed. One was local, one was bracketed as Coventry. There were two numbers for Dr Lombard which Kerr took to be firstly work and secondly home. The reverse was true for what he assumed was the Kents' entry: a single line which simply read 'Annie and John' with no accompanying surname. Melissa Woolstone, the woman who'd gone to New Zealand, was listed too, except that she didn't appear, as might have been expected, under W but in the middle of the Gs. Harvey had added her details after crossing out the still legible name, address and telephone number of someone called Laura Gregory. The address and the number rang no bells but there was something about the name itself which prodded irritatingly at his brain. It was probably nothing, or nothing important, but he put in a call to the incident room just in case. He'd learnt from bitter experience that – for a policeman – checked was always better than unchecked.

Jacobson took the call from Coventry in his own office. He'd forgotten that Nelson worked there. In all truth he'd forgotten about Nelson. Yet they'd been as thick as thieves for ten days. Jacobson, Nelson and the Yorkshireman. Hutton, that was him. They'd all been on the Met's suspect profiling course together, a mob of provincial grannies learning a new jargon for sucking eggs.

'No trace of chummie, Frank. Nice little set-up too. Detached house, good area. The old lady across the street reckons she saw him being driven off in a taxi around nine on Monday morning. His own car's locked up in his garage, a red BMW – 518, newish. No sign of passports, bank books or that kind of thing in the house and no suitcases either. There's also a Mrs JA Mitchell listed at the same address. She's quite well known in the area as it turns out, runs some kind of local road safety campaign. Apparently, their little boy was killed in a traffic accident three years ago. Drunk driver, hit and run – the usual mess. The thing is the old lady says she hasn't seen Mrs M for a month. Just Mitchell himself back occasionally to check on the house. My lads have got their hands full as usual but I've left one officer on door-to-door to see if any other nosy neighbours can corroborate. Give me your mobile number and I'll get straight through to you if we turn up anything else.'

Jacobson gave him the number and thanked him. He suggested they meet up for a drink sometime but he knew in his heart of hearts he'd never get around to it. Not for its own sake anyway, not unless it involved the pursuit of some case or other. At the end of the corridor, he pushed open the glass-panelled door which was boldly but falsely labelled 'PULL' and headed back downstairs to the incident room.

Pub brawl equals men, domestic violence or lost kiddies equals women: because of the outdated division of labour which still applied in the force, DC Emma Smith knew that she would have recognised Laura Gregory's name and location instantly. Annoyingly, because she already knew who Laura Gregory was, she probably wouldn't have checked her name on the Police National Computer as DC Williams, who'd taken the call from DS Kerr, had just routinely done. In which case, she conceded – although only to herself – the unexpected criminal record would have remained buried in the computer's memory instead of splashing itself in amber letters across the sweat-stained screen of the incident room's main terminal.

... 4956433/ac L. Gregory/ Active Series 321>/ ... born Laura Fielding Gregory. Convictions: 03/03/94, Affray, Serious Assault on Police Officer, Resisting Arrest, Anti-Abortion Counter Demonstration, Westminster, sentenced 3 mnths, Holloway ... Last known occupation: Women's Refuge Organiser, Crowby ...

She pressed the printscreen keys and then scrolled through the entry again. She'd met Laura Gregory maybe half a dozen times and she'd never had any cause to doubt her reputation as a dedicated, capable worker. 'But' – she sensed herself mouthing the word – she'd never really liked her, had always suspected that the dislike was mutual. The refuge viewpoint, which Laura had taken pains to express to her on more than one occasion, was that the police never did enough, were all sexist themselves anyway. As for policewomen, at worst they colluded in patri-archal oppression, at best they were the misguided victims of official tokenism.

She logged off the terminal and picked up the hard copy from the printer's paper tray. She would never have guessed at the violence which had lain hidden only a few years back in Laura Gregory's past. But the revelation didn't, she realised, seem totally out of step with her own first-hand impressions. Her gut feeling had always been that in the world according to Laura there was no scope for compromise: you belonged to the sisterhood or you didn't, you were either for her or against her.

Wordsworth Avenue wasn't the most anti-police street on the estate known as Son of the Bronx. Nor was Son of the Bronx as hostile an area as the Bronx itself, two miles further out of town. Even so, DC Barber wouldn't have wanted to be out here in the badlands on his own. He locked the car carefully, glad for once of DC Hume's broad-shouldered company. Mick Hume looked on huffily. Checking out toe-rag Geordie's alibi wasn't his concept of a high-priority task. He'd said exactly that to DS Kerr but all he'd got back was the official line. 'He found the body or says he did, Mick. It's standard procedure, you know that.' Of course he knew it. But knowing it didn't mean he agreed with it. As far as he was concerned, they couldn't leave the useless little twat banged up long enough.

The front garden of George McCulloch's home was the final resting place for the shell of a burnt-out Escort and a selection of old tyres:

commercial, tractor, saloon – all of them looked totally useless. Bob McCulloch loomed up in the doorway just as they reached the front step.

'Ah thought ah'd tidy it up a bit while ah wis here.'

The big man, bigger even than Hume, showed them into an interior that was part disaster area, part spick and span.

'Ah'm keepin' an eye oan the place while Geordie assists yir inquiries.'

Hume came in last, pulled the door shut behind him.

'You'll be starting a Neighbourhood Watch next.'

'Ah've heard worse ideas. There's some good people live here, contrary tae popular belief.'

Hume's reply was a silent sneer. It was left to Barber to play the diplomat.

'Point taken, Mr McCulloch, no offence.'

Bob was Geordie's elder brother. He drove long-distance, his record was minimal, he wasn't even a heavy drinker. He claimed he'd spent all of Sunday with his brother and Jacobson was giving the claim credence.

'Ah drove him over tae the crematorium in the afternoon. Flowers for the garden of remembrance. After tea, we were in the Poets. Half the street must've seen him. We came back here about eleven. He could hardly walk never mind anything else – temazepam on top o' the bevvy.'

McCulloch shook his head, his expression a

mixture of exasperation and regret.

'We watched a couple of videos. Geordie crashed oot on the couch – must've been after one. He wis still deid tae the world the next morning.'

Barber thanked him for his time, stalled him on the nature of the charges facing his witless brother. There would, he knew, be several reliable witnesses in the public bar of the Poets: reliable in the restricted sense that they seemed to more or less live in the place, drinking themselves steadily into numbness, swapping stolen goods, betting their giros on interminable games of pool. They'd all have seen Geordie's state, his temporary unfitness for any kind of misdemeanour. A couple of preliminary statements – half an hour's work, say – and they could be on their way. Even Hume looked less aggrieved until, headed for the car, he tripped over the biggest tyre in the garden and banged his head on the side of what was left of the Escort.

He turned round to remonstrate with McCulloch but the exiled Glaswegian had already closed the door and switched his heavy-duty vacuum cleaner back on.

Emma Smith had been about to start on the list of minor companies when British Airways returned her call. She'd started with the big carriers as a matter of course but she hadn't really expected to get a result from them. If you wanted to slip quietly out the country, you wouldn't want to register the fact in the databases of a major airline. Or so she'd thought: David Mitchell looked to have done exactly that. According to BA, someone using Mitchell's passport had boarded a mid-morning flight from Birmingham International to Amsterdam Schiphol on Monday. Someone using Mitchell's name and using his Coventry address had booked and paid for a single business class seat a fortnight earlier via the Crowby branch of Thomas Cook.

Jacobson passed her a cup of instant coffee mixed with powdered milk and put a teabag in the cup intended for DC Williams. Neither of them had worked with him before today, neither of them really knew what to make of this reversal of the normal etiquette. Jacobson removed the teabag and threw it in the wastebin. Williams grabbed at the cup before Jacobson had time to pass it over to him. After the call from BA, the incident room, with only the three of them present, had gone so unusually quiet they could hear the gurgling of the radiators. Williams was on phone duty but even the Looney Tunes contingent, who could always be relied upon to clog up the phone lines on the first day of a murder case, seemed to be taking a break from their usual string of hoax calls, false accusations and manifestations of religious mania. Jacobson picked up his own cup and walked over to the window.

In daylight, there was a view across the pedestrian precinct to the row of sturdy oaks in front of the town hall. But right now, all he had to look at, without pressing his nose to the glass, was the reflection of the room staring back at him and his own, dourly shadowed face. His problem, as he saw it, was that outside the country could mean outside his hands. It would need Detective Chief Superintendent Chivers to liaise with Scotland Yard to liaise with Interpol. In that context, Chivvy himself would only be the messenger boy.

He needed to rehearse a new line for official consumption: regardless of where the suspect had got to, investigating the full background to the case still remained the responsibility of the local side – or something to that general effect. He decided to let DC Smith drive him over to the crime scene on her way to the hostel; that ought to give him the time he needed to think the thing through.

The Crowby Women's Refuge was in a street of solid Victorian houses on the other side of the Fellows Memorial Park from the Riverside Hotel. Emma rang the bell at the side of a thick, heavily-secured door. She was no stranger here in pursuit of statements which were often withdrawn or denied in court: women 'reconciled' to violent partners or content, having escaped, to let sleeping dogs lie. A tired-looking young woman answered the door and showed her through to the downstairs room which functioned as the refuge's office. It was several minutes before Laura Gregory herself put in an appearance. She was barefooted and wrapped in a long, white bathrobe. It was hard to know whether she'd been getting ready for bed or whether she'd already been asleep and had been woken up.

There was no offer of coffee, no preliminaries, no option but to take the direct approach.

'The reason I'm here is that we understand you knew Roger Harvey well. As I expect you've seen or heard in the news—'

'Yes, I've heard. Bad news. He was a nice guy. But I don't know what I can tell you, it must be over a year since I last saw him.'

She slurred some of her words and her breath smelt strongly of whisky. Emma asked her how closely she'd known Roger Harvey.

'Close enough. We were lovers of a kind for about a year. Perhaps I'd see him once or twice a week. He was absorbed in his work, independent, not looking for any serious involvement and neither was I.'

'How did you meet him?'

'In the traditional way. He picked me up in a bar. I liked the sound of his voice mainly. That and his way of – Christ, why am I telling you all this? It's not as if you actually care, is it?'

There were half a dozen stock answers to the question but Laura Gregory looked unlikely to buy any of them. Instead Emma asked her whether she'd shared any mutual friends or acquaintances with Harvey.

'No, not really. We weren't involved with each other in that kind of way. To be frank, it was just a sexual thing. He did drag me over to these friends of his in Wynarth – the Kents – a couple of times, but eventually he worked it out that I'm not ideal dinner party material.'

'There was a man called Mitchell, a neighbour—'

'It's news to me. I didn't think he knew any of his neighbours.'

'And after a while – nearly a year – you just stopped seeing him?'

'It was no big deal. He started going out with some woman who worked in the university library.'

'I see. How did you react to that?'

'Come off it, Detective Smith, you sound like a trainee counsellor – I wasn't mad with jealousy if that's what you were hoping for. It was simply a question of my standards, expectations. Serial monogamy, if you like. If I'd taken up with someone else I wouldn't have expected to carry on with Roger. It was just a pleasant arrangement that ran its course.'

'So you parted on good terms?'

'If that's how you want to put it. It really wasn't that important to me. *Men* aren't that important to me. If they behave themselves, they have their uses. Otherwise . . .'

She produced a lighter and a packet of Superkings from the pocket of her bathrobe. Her fingers were shaking as she took out a cigarette and managed with some difficulty to light it. Emma Smith studied Laura Gregory's face, noticed the bleary redness which clouded her ash-blue eyes. It was natural enough to be in need of a stiffener or two if you'd just learned that an old flame had been brutally murdered. But only, she reflected, if you still cared a little for him, still felt something. If Roger Harvey had really only been a convenient, no-strings sexual partner, then why the insistence on his fidelity? Then there was the new and unexpected knowledge of the conviction for assault. An assault serious enough to have landed her a stretch inside. It had been August when Mitchell moved in so it was credible that Laura Gregory had never heard of him – but only if she was telling the truth when she'd said she hadn't seen Harvey in the last year.

She put away her notebook, made it clear that she didn't intend to carry on her questioning for much longer. The Ahmeds had overheard an argument between three voices, one of them probably female. She had only one important question left to ask.

'One other thing. I need to know your where-abouts on Sunday evening. It's a routine question in this sort of case.'

Laura Gregory exhaled a deep lungful of

smoke and raised her eyebrows in mock surprise.

'I'm sure. As routine as forensic inaccuracies and doctored statements. Fortunately for me, I was right here on sleep-over duty just like tonight – and I can prove it too.'

Kerr gave Jacobson a guided tour of Roger Harvey's flat, pointing out the highlights of his discoveries. Jacobson showed considerably more interest than he'd done himself in the pile of videos stacked on a shelf near the television set, even kneeling down to examine them in detail.

'*Les Enfants du Paradis, Diva, Gazon Maudit . . .*'

He read aloud several of the mainly foreign titles, shaking his head as if in response to some gloomy, private preoccupation. Kerr didn't trouble him further by asking what was on his mind. The soco appeared in the doorway to announce he'd finished in David Mitchell's place and Jacobson got up stiffly, rubbing his knees. Kerr led the way out.

Unless you wanted to count a copy of *Computer Weekly* on the kitchen table and a carton of semi-skimmed milk curdling in the fridge, Mitchell's temporary residence appeared to lack any clues to his personality or lifestyle. The furniture was smart, modern, but chosen with no one particular in mind. There were no letters or documents anywhere. When Mitchell had left Crowby, it looked as if he hadn't planned on returning.

Kerr passed through to the bedroom. There were no clothes in the wardrobe. On a white bedside cabinet, a small clock radio still showed the correct time. Nine forty-two. Kerr looked more closely. The radio and alarm was also a cassette player. He pulled open the top drawer of the cabinet. It was empty except for a cassette tape, a Sony C90. Kerr took it out and read the four words which had been neatly handwritten on the white, stuck-on label: Van Morrison, *Astral Weeks*.

Around midnight, a bellyful of fruitless door-to-door plodding under his belt, under the belts of everyone on the team, Jacobson wearily closed his own front door behind him. There was only a tide of junk mail on his unhoovered carpet but the green light twinkled on his answerphone.

'Hi, Dad. It's me. I'm headed north on Sunday. I thought maybe I could change trains in Crowby, maybe catch a meal with you in the evening.'

Sally! He passed through the lounge, slinging his jacket un-neatly in a corner. In the kitchen, he rinsed a glass clean and got plenty of ice. At least, he thought, the very worst had past, the five long years when they'd scarcely heard from her. 'This family is dysfunctional! I don't want anything more to do with it.' In Sally's eyes, the sins of the absent father had been compounded by those of the clinging over-protective mother. They were, he knew, standard complaints between that generation and his, yet he'd never contested the analysis, never denied its truth. It was just the way it was, the way it had been. He poured out a generous measure, walked back through to the lounge again. Now there was a sort of peace, a truce of non-intrusion, of inter-mittent contacts. He'd actually heard more from her since his bust-up with his wife – her big battles had always been with Janice.

As the video rewound, the last minutes of the late news recapped on the usual nightmares, tragedies, official bungles. He loosened his collar, eased off his shoes. Click. The tape was ready – assuming he'd set it up for the right channel and hadn't stored himself an hour of game show and soap instead of the programme he wanted to see.

He'd been hooked on the early civilisations even before he'd taken his Open University degree (a futile effort to raise his chances of promotion in the days when he'd still believed it was worth trying for). The earlier the better: the trouble with the OU's courses was that they'd really only gone in for Greece and Rome. Jacobson wasn't as turned on by the latecomers. He wanted to know about Babylon more than Egypt, about Sumer more than anywhere. He drank a deep mouthful of the fiery-cool Glenfiddich, watched a hot sun shimmering on the screen. 'Art in early Sumeria delighted in the depiction of everyday scenes and activities.' If the commentary so far had only stated the obvious, at any rate it was accurate enough. As far as Jacobson knew, the degeneration into royal portraiture and glorification had come later – after the warlike Akkadians hit town.

The researchers were grubbing around in sand and rock. The talk was 3500BC, 2400BC, vast sweeps of population and migration. The killing of Dr Roger Harvey was an infinitesimally small affair by comparison. They were using actors to recreate the daily routines in a grain store. He watched the ledger man painstakingly tabling his accounts in the sweaty heat, tried to imagine the reality of lives which had been over and gone five thousand years before his own. Like everybody else, the Sumerians had had their one shot at wine, sex, sunsets, the breeze across the water, the sharpness of olives. Like everybody else, they'd spent too much time counting the grain, worrying about the boss, paying the piper.

He took another mouthful, noticed the snaking lines which the melting icewater made as it fused into the whisky. The trouble with a murder inquiry was that there was no telling in advance when he might be able to snatch some time off-duty, no telling when it would all be finally over. But he promised himself he'd make the date with Sally somehow, even if he had to go AWOL.

Murder or no murder, he didn't get the chance to dine out with his grown-up daughter every day, to spend a couple of hours as if he was an ordinary citizen, with no case to solve and nothing to prove.

Kerr stared restlessly into the darkness. Cathy was already in bed when he'd got back, had pretended to be asleep when he got in beside her. Now she really was sleeping, her breathing deep and even. For some reason it made him think of waves breaking on the shore of a calm ocean.

He reminded himself that the row wouldn't last, that they never did. It was only one of the patterns their lives had somehow fallen into, unhappy but familiar. In a day or so she'd allow herself to be cajoled, made to laugh. 'It's always good when we make up': the kind of thing she'd say later.

He ran his hand down the warmth of her back. He'd never tired of her body. Its very familiarity excited him, its neatness, snugness. It occurred to him that they could carry on like this for years. Most people did, with or without kids, chasing the illusion of permanence, changelessness. They called it commitment, claimed it as an adult choice. But what it really amounted to was settling down, settling for what you had, settling for what you could get. Cocooned. Right now it felt to Kerr like the exact opposite of grown-upness.

Still sleeping, Cathy turned towards him unconsciously, instinctually. He held her for a moment and kissed her mouth. Then he turned away, closing his eyes.

By the time it got to one am in Crowby, it was already two am in Amsterdam. David Mitchell drew back the curtain and peered into the wetness over Dam Square, the rain falling in sheets between the Royal Palace and the war memorial. There was very nearly no one in sight. No late-night revellers, no drugged-out derelicts. Only a solitary street cleaner sneaking a quick cigarette break in a doorway, his road-sweeping machine motionless on the edge of the pavement. It was Mitchell's fourth night in the Hotel Krasnapolsky and if everything went according to plan it would be his last.

He let the curtain drop and lay back down on the bed. He was wearing only an unbuttoned shirt and black boxer shorts. He adjusted his pillow to a more comfortable angle and pressed pause on the remote control.

The protagonist had the woman bent over the car bonnet. His right hand held down her neck, pressing her face into the shiny blue surface. Her dress was loose, red, flouncy. With the picture frozen, you could see his other hand, thumb inside the knickers, hooking them down. Another press of his own thumb and the sequence replayed. Tussling, muffled screams, then he's in

75

her, really giving it to her. You could see her stop struggling, starting to enjoy it. He's slapping her arse as he fucks her. 'You behave better now, eh?' 'Yes, oh yes.' Another slap, another gasp, the woman's face in close-up, bright red lips against blue metal: 'Please don't stop, please, please.'

All week Mitchell had wanted to hit one of the city's hot spots, pick up some real-life action. But he was intent on lying low, following Kolb's instructions to the letter. He'd be able to take his pick soon anyway. Hong Kong, Bangkok, Sun City maybe. He leant over the side of the bed, examined the contents of the bag. Beer, whisky, vodka? Another beer, mate. Another beer was totally, definitely, requisite. Re-que-zeet. He ran the sounds around his mouth, savouring the resonance of the 'zeet'.

He sat back up, drinking straight from the can. The woman was on her knees now, eyes starry, oiling her abductor's tanned back by the pool. A plot was being hatched. Something about going fifty-fifty, getting the husband out of the picture. Another hiatus before another coupling; Mitchell wasn't bothered, wasn't in any immediate rush. He could watch this rubbish all night if he felt like it, keep himself rat-arsed all night if he chose to. From now on he'd be doing exactly, precisely, whatever he wanted to do. The days of taking other perspectives, other interests, into account were done with. Harvey, Jean, Crowby, Coventry: Kolb would get here in the afternoon and the past would be irrevocably buried, finished.

The movie cut jerkily to a motel bedroom, the woman naked in the shower. Mitchell reached for the remote control again, spilled beer down his shirt and pants, felt coldness spreading over his stomach. He turned over on his wet guts and fell into a snore-ridden sleep.

Friday

Chapter Four

Jacobson held his B and H covertly behind his back until the whole team was in the room and the door was fully closed. Better safe than sorry: the cells and interview rooms were now the only parts of the building where smoking was officially tolerated and it was exactly the time of day when the Health and Safety inquisitors liked to go corridor-prowling in search of nicotine-fingered heretics.

Jacobson knew from experience that an upbeat morning briefing was vital to the progress of an investigation. For one thing, it was the only occasion which guaranteed the simultaneous presence of every officer involved. There were entire courses at Hendon devoted to the art of this kind of motivational meeting. Endless, wearisome afternoons when traffic inspectors from Swindon got to play Knacker of the Yard and any real CID kept their heads down, tried to keep their faces straight. But Crowby was real-life not role-play and right now he faced the basic problem that there was virtually sod all new to be said. Only politicians and chief constables could take nothing and make it sound like something. Jacobson knew he would never be either.

He took a deep draw before he started to speak. Admittedly, Laura Gregory's criminal record was an unexpected development that might lead somewhere. He wanted Kerr to talk to the Kents again – find out what they knew about her – and he would ask Emma Smith to help him with the details of the assault itself. But most of the team would have heard about this line of inquiry the previous evening, would have weighed it gloomily in the balance against David Mitchell's successful exit out of the country. Which really only left him with the laboratory confirmation that Harvey's skull had been bludgeoned with a solid brass object and that said object must have been around two to three pounds in weight. It was hardly an earth-shattering revelation but at least it was just in, fresh. There had even been traces in the wounds which would positively identify the murder weapon should it ever be recovered.

But *would* it be? He took a second draw, less from need than as a delaying tactic. The search in the fields had yielded nothing so far which remotely fitted the forensic parameters and only the Ahmeds had reported anything out of the ordinary in the small hours of Monday morning.

If – as it seemed – chummie didn't panic after the event, the chances of finding the weapon stowed carelessly in the vicinity were frankly zilch. This was a seriously bad outcome for Sergeant Ince's commitment to providing his uniformed plods with infinite overtime opportunities. But Jacobson couldn't see any other reasonable inference to make from the available facts.

He scanned the faces looking towards him – some alert, some still sleepy, all of them waiting. He'd start with that then, get the worst out of the way first:

'You can have another morning, Ince, old son. Complete the sweep through the wood and then we'll need to scrap it. Upstairs are going to shit on a big production for a single man, no family, no apparent connection to other offences.'

Kerr made a detour to the Wynarth Arms on his way to the Kents. It was a thin chance but if Harvey and the Kents had been Thursday night regulars, there might be some background to be gleaned. A weak, wintry sun reached through the high arched window in the main lounge and picked on the flecks of cigarette ash hovering in the air. An original Wurlitzer, its sound boosted and routed through hidden speakers, sent 'In Dreams' across the room at a volume close to distortion. It was as if the pub itself had a hangover. Roy Orbison always made Kerr think of drunks anyway. Years ago: down the club with his father, some singer in a cheap suit murdering the words as well as the tune.

Stevie R was on top of one end of the long, wooden bar, nailing in place the black and white banner which promised 'THE WYNARTH ARMS BLUES FEST KICKS ASS'. Underneath the 'W', Linda, Mrs R, was setting up the till.

'Mr and Mrs Richardson? Can you spare a minute?'

He showed them his warrant card, watched the smile on their faces freeze halfway. He'd only been a customer here before. Now they'd always know him as a policeman.

'Yeah, he got in here now and again. I said that to Linda last night when I saw his photograph in the paper. I'd never caught his name though. Usually we'd see him with John Kent and his lady.'

'Last Thursday?'

'Nah, but the week before I'm sure.'

'But you'd call the Kents themselves regulars then?'

'John Kent anyway, part of our early evening trade most nights. Mrs Kent is another one we usually only see on Thursday nights. It's our best gig night what with the old r and b stuff.'

'In Dreams' faded, Question Mark and the Mysterians were the next selection up.

'Ninety-Six T—': but Linda pressed a switch under the counter, cut them dead.

'It said on the radio this morning that the police had ruled out burglary as a motive.'

It was a preamble, not a question. Stevie glowered.

'What you on about, girl?'

'Come on, Steve. We've got to tell him – there's been a murder!'

'Mr Richardson?'

He was probably too old for his Megadeath T-shirt, certainly too old for his hairstyle, maybe too old for his wife. Kerr knew he wasn't really going to hold back. He was just a big kid who wanted to be coaxed, taken seriously.

'Oh, all right then. Can't do us no harm – I hope.'

They told him they'd never really noticed the geezer they now knew had been Harvey before that night nor the Kents pretty much. It had only been in the last six months that John Kent had joined the late-at-the-office crew. This had been more like a year ago, maybe a bit more. Another Thursday night, but quiet for once and late – after last orders.

'They were at the table over there. John Kent and his lady and Harvey with another. Bit of a looker, no more than twenty-five.'

'Then this woman walks straight in, straight across. She pulls a Stanley knife, going for Harvey like.'

'Linda saw it first. I got over there quick but I think she was more out for the drama of it really.

The four of them were just sat there, stunned. She's waving the bloody thing around like she's demented. I can still picture it: yellow handle. Then she seems just to go quiet. Puts it back in her bag, says you're not fucking worth it and walks back out.'

'You didn't call—'

'There's no actual injuries, no damage. Harvey's saying no police, like it's a domestic thing. So there don't seem any point.'

Linda had the best description but it didn't add up to much. Medium height, medium thirties, medium brown hair. Still there was always Stevie R's belief in his own abilities:

'Yeah, I know it's a crap description but if I saw her again I'd know her. That's all I can say.'

Annie Kent shivered a little as she swept the leaves from the base of the Green Man. She glanced back at the house, caught a glimpse of John Kent as he moved past the kitchen window. She hadn't slept well and now she wondered whether her husband had slept at all. She didn't expect it could be easy for him, having just lost his oldest, closest friend. She raked the leaves into a black bin liner and then, straightening up, ran her free hand along the contours of the Green Man's familiar, rugged features.

Altogether there were four of her sculptures in the garden. The Fire Snake coiled its way around the branches of the beech tree. The Enchanted

Frog waited in vain for his princess's kiss by the side of the pond while Pan himself piped the way to the conservatory. Her idea had been that eventually the Green Man would be joined by his Green Woman. They would lurk together, only partially visible, luring unwary hearts into the unkempt bushes which she'd intentionally encouraged to run wild at the foot of the garden.

She picked up the bag of leaves and started back up the path. She knew only too well that it was hardly an original concept, would happily tell anyone interested enough to ask that she'd pinched the idea wholesale from an exhibition she'd visited in London five or six years previously. It was really just something that she thought would look good, something she could achieve within her dwindling technique. If she'd ever thought of herself as an artist – and she wasn't sure that she ever had, not seriously – it was an idea she no longer clung to. It wasn't even that she could say she'd put John's career before any possible career of her own. It was simply the way things had turned out, the specific cards which life had dealt up for her. As she reached the top of the path, she saw him suddenly at the window again. He was looking towards her, waving her to come in: a faint, wary smile on an ageing, anxious face.

Her eyes were red and her hair hadn't been brushed but Kerr felt no cause to revise his original sex-object rating of Mrs Kent. They sat down in the front room while John Kent resumed his interrupted conversation with the funeral directors from the phone in the hall. Kerr asked her why they hadn't thought to mention anything about Laura Gregory the day before. Surely they could see it might be relevant?

'Well, yes, perhaps we ought to have said something but I just don't seem to be able to think straight since this happened.'

Beatrice Webb, a border collie a long way from home, slept on the rug regardless.

'I'm sure it was just an empty threat anyway. An expression of feelings. You can't really think that—'

Kerr *could* think it – now that he knew that the same Laura Gregory who'd had a go at a policewoman had also pulled a Stanley knife on Roger Harvey – but he kept his thoughts to himself.

'It's a matter of building up a background picture at this stage, that's all. I take it you're a friend of Ms Gregory's?'

'Well, scarcely. Roger brought her to dinner a couple of times while he was seeing her. Also, there used to be a strong women's group in Wynarth though it's sort of fallen apart recently. She spoke to us a couple of times about her work at the refuge but I think she felt we were timewasters, middle-class bitches indulging ourselves.'

'So when was the last time you saw or heard from her?'

'That *was* it, that night in the Wynarth Arms. It was the first time we'd seen Roger with Melissa. A lovely girl. For a time, we thought maybe this is the one.'

Annie looked into space, stroked the top of Beatrice Webb's head.

'But she's in New Zealand now. I think I told you yesterday.'

John Kent paused in the doorway.

'Assuming the coroner gives his permission today, the burial can go ahead on Monday.'

'I can't see a problem, Mr, ehm, John. There's a complete autopsy report and there's been a formal identification. The inquest should be adjourned fairly swiftly.'

Autopsies, identification: the living man become dead meat for official processing. The tears welled up on Annie Kent's face until they reached bursting point, until she was crying out loud, keening.

Kerr got up, careful with his feet and the dog, feeling he should be out of the way. Somehow all three of them – John Kent, Kerr, Beatrice Webb – were moving in and out of the doorway at the same time. A pile of hardbacks toppled. Kent went to pick them up but Kerr nudged him towards his wife, bent to pick them up himself. He saw that they were all copies of the same book: on each dust-jacket, a nineteenth-century navvy with his clay-pipe and crumpled hat walked along a towpath. Kent started to say something to him, his words difficult to follow against the background of Annie's sobbing.

'My magnum opus. Ten years in the making and remaindered after six months. Still it got me into canals, narrowboats. I can't really complain.'

The incident room had got a lot noisier since the night before. Emma Smith pressed the receiver tight to her ear. She'd encountered a major piece of luck connected to Laura Gregory's violent past. The senior welfare officer she'd contacted at the Met had not only been a junior staff counsellor back in '94, she'd been the very one who'd dealt with the policewoman attacked by Right On Laura. Better than that, she'd kept in touch with her after she'd quit the force. The attackee's name was Marilyn Wright and she'd traded in a flat in Nunhead for a cottage in Cornwall, somewhere near Tintagel.

Emma tried to picture her but failed to match an image to the quiet, unhurried voice on the other end of the telephone.

'Detective Smith? Yes, this is Marilyn Wright.'

She'd been a policewoman once but now who was she? And what would you do in Cornwall all day? Collect driftwood on the beach, she supposed, or make corn dollies.

'Please, call me Emma. I'm really sorry to put you through this.'

'It's OK, really. They sent a young chap over from Tintagel to let me know what it was about.'

Even that bit had gone smoothly. The local bobby had been happy to make a house call, reassure her that the interview wouldn't be a hoax or malicious.

'Fine. I want you to be as quick or as long as you need.'

There was silence down the line and then Emma thought she heard a deep intake of breath before the woman spoke again.

'It seemed easy enough at first. My eighth demo plus I'd done the Riot City training twice. By the time it happened, the pro-life people had already packed up and there'd been no arrests. Then some of the counter-demonstrators decided to sit down on the road – trying to ensure publicity or something – while the rest are standing watching from the pavement. We move in and start carting them into the wagons. Heavy cows some of them but there's still no real aggro. I go in to lift another one and I don't remember too much after that. Just this voice booming, "Don't you fucking touch her." I'm seeing black, red, hazy figures moving around me. Then it's as if I'm falling for ever.'

Marilyn Wright paused again. Emma imagined her looking at the sea through her cottage window, arranging flowers or stroking a docile cat: a policewoman who'd moved a million light years away from policing.

'They had it all on the police cameras. She'd just run off the pavement, came at me with some kind of cosh. They said in court she didn't even know the woman I was trying to arrest. Some of the other demonstrators gave evidence against her.'

'How long did it take you to get over the injuries?'

'I was in and out of hospitals for two, three years. All the feeling came back in the end. I can swim now, run even. Sometimes I can pretend she did me a favour – everything I do now, even just the idea of living somewhere like this. In a way, it all stems from then.'

Even down the phone line, her final pause felt like a shudder:

'But no sane person would have done what she did.'

It was almost lunchtime when Jacobson finally traced Dr Colin Scott, the author of Laura Gregory's psychiatric referral. He was about to head upstairs, make the call in his own office, when DC Mick Hume, his lugubrious face very nearly animated, handed him a fax still hot from the machine.

'Take a look at this guv.'

Jacobson grabbed the spare corner of a desk and studied the details. The fingerprints lifted from Harvey's flat had been sent off to the Criminal Records Office for cross-checking. It was a process which used to take days, even weeks, but now computerisation had cut the waiting time to hours. Jacobson hadn't been wildly optimistic. The most he'd expected had been a confirmation of George McCulloch's sweaty presence. Geordie had developed a reckless, careless streak since Sylvie had OD'd, almost like he wanted to be caught. It would be just like him to break into Harvey's place without bothering with gloves. But there was no trace of Geordie. What there *was* instead was Annie Kent. It seemed that Mrs Kent had a five-year-old conviction for shoplifting in Debenhams and had copped three months' probation. Not to mention being bound over for a year on a related charge of resisting arrest. He asked Hume – who immediately looked less chipper – to dig out the local records of the case. Anything more than two or three years old was still stored manually: it might only be a ten minute job but it could just as easily take two hours.

The shabby corridor along the fourth floor of the Divisional building was a haven of peace after the incident room. Yesterday, Jacobson thought, must have been the crank callers' day off: they were certainly making up for it today. He found himself stopping at the lift, even though he knew he ought to make an effort and take the stairs. So Mrs Kent was Known To The Police. Jesus! Maybe he should run Vice Chancellor Croucher's name through the Police

National Computer just to be on the safe side. He got out the lift, pulled open the PUSH door and retreated into his office.

To his surprise he got straight through to Scott inside three rings.

'Another bloody academic.' Jacobson had still to accommodate himself to the sensitivity of the modern telephone. If Scott was coming across like a shirty bastard, it was probably because he'd caught the remark.

'Yes, Inspector. I remember the case well. It was in my last year of treading the wards.'

'Your report recommended considerable leniency given the severe consequences of the offence.'

'I stand fully by my recommendations. There was no doubt that a prison sentence was merited but the case was, I think, better served by a short period of custody and ongoing counselling. My understanding is that she's now wholly integrated into a useful life of service to the community.'

Jacobson swivelled in his chair. There were times when he sensed a conspiracy of events to switch him to the *Daily Telegraph*.

'She put a good policewoman off the force.'

'You have to realise her stepfather was remarrying, the second time her mother had been deserted. She'd just had significant rejection in her own life. There'd been some meddling with drugs also. Something snaps, it sometimes does. She was fully under the impression she'd attacked a male officer. My assessment was that it was a temporary breakdown. Underneath I found no evidence of permanent instability.'

Jacobson grudgingly thanked him for his time. He let his temper cool for five minutes and then took the stairs all the way down to the ground floor. It would hardly qualify as aerobic exercise but he persuaded himself it was a start, kind of. He nodded to the desk sergeant who was processing George McCulloch into the care of his brother, Bob. The sergeant was emphasizing the importance of the R73 form.

'Make sure he doesn't lose it. His brief'll need it if he wants a copy of the interview tape. It could go in his favour that he reported the body straight away.'

Jacobson halted for a moment by the side of the revolving doors, buttoning up his coat. Geordie stuck the pink form into an inside pocket easily enough but then he had trouble getting his hand back out. He was white-faced, shivering. Jacobson looked hard at him. When he'd been Geordie's age, junkies could be counted in a few thousands; exotic bohemians who romanticized their withdrawal symptoms as cold turkey, even argued their addiction as a type of radical politics. Now heroin was more British than fish and chips and scrotes like Geordie only knew that they felt like shit when they couldn't get a hit.

Bob McCulloch caught sight of Jacobson. He

shook his head and let out a sigh through pursed lips. Jacobson recalled the times in the past when Bob had invented a problem with the surety, had deliberately left Geordie banged up. By now he must have lost count of the number of times he'd seen his brother straighten out that way or some other way. Each time swearing he would stay clean, each time – inevitably – going back. Jacobson was halfway down the outside steps when the McCullochs caught up with him. Bob McCulloch seemed to have read his thoughts.

'He lasted out three months wance. But mair often it's three days or three hours.'

Geordie said nothing, was maybe used to being talked about in the third person – like a senile OAP or a stroke victim.

'It used to be if Sylvie didn't talk Geordie intae it, Geordie would talk Sylvie intae it.'

Jacobson didn't need convincing. Nowadays, he thought, Geordie just persuaded himself.

Bob zipped Geordie's jacket up, punched him lightly on the shoulder.

'Come oan, let's get you hame. Some of us have got jobs tae go to.'

The Laura Gregory conference convened in Mr Behar's. Above their heads, the elephant god Ganesha, patron saint of scholars and general bringer of good fortune, frolicked with his handmaidens.

Chicken zhalfraji, off the bone, plus 'Behar's

Special' pillau rice with bhindi bajii and a pesh-wari nan on the side: Kerr and DC Smith had stuck resolutely to the business lunch but Jacobson just said yes to an à la carte menu. It was agreed though that they'd help him out with the generous selection of sundries he'd ordered. He talked Smith into an experiment with Kingfisher lager but Kerr continued his bid for Perrier's Policeman of the Month award. Like the port at a chief constables' dinner, the formulation of problems passed round the table in turn.

Emma Smith spooned cucumber raita on to her plate, contrasted Laura Gregory's possession of both a motive and a relevant history with David Michell's apparent lack of either. Jacobson broke off a piece of poppadum laden with hot lime pickle, held it poised across the table.

'So what we're left with is this. Mitchell has no apparent motive but does a highly coincidental and conspicuous runner. Laura Gregory, on the other hand, *has* a possible motive if she went on nursing her jealousy against Harvey. She's also, as we now know, got a history of violence and mental disturbance. The problem is that – unlike Mitchell – she's stayed put in Crowby and looks to have a rock-solid alibi.'

Kerr prodded the ice cubes in his glass, wondered if there could be some connection between the two suspects. It was a point Emma had already considered.

'There's nothing to suggest their paths have

ever crossed. Given her record, you'd expect to pick up any prints in the cross-check so it looks as if she could be telling the truth about not having visited Harvey in months.'

Jacobson played nasty guy/nice guy with his tongue. The zhalfraji's fiercest chilli preceded the peshwari's almond-sweetness preceded a clean mouthful of lager preceded more of the chilli.

'Nothing so far, anyway. If Laura's our girl she did a good job of covering her tracks after the event but then the same could be said of David Mitchell in reverse. The forensics found Harvey's thumbprints in Mitchell's kitchen and it's more than likely they'll find Mitchell's in Harvey's gaff once they know what they're looking for. If you're worried about print evidence, it's always best to top a mate.'

Behar's culinary energies were quite reasonably reserved for the full-price menu. Kerr stabbed a prawn out of a mild curry sauce, began to regret his choice of the business option.

'That's actually what bothers me about Mitchell altogether. The whole style of the killing says loss of control, sudden frenzy not pre-meditation – yet this character's booking his flight a whole fortnight earlier, enrolling himself on a course to cover the fact he's about to skip the country.'

Jacobson smiled, spoke, broke the formal sequence of circling contributions.

'Ian, old son, murder isn't an either/or commodity except in the simplest cases. A murder could be planned for weeks, months and still the killer acts like an animal when he – or she – finally does the business.'

Jacobson broke off more poppadum, Emma spooned more cucumber raita on to her plate. A meeting ostensibly focused on Laura Gregory was running wide of its remit. Kerr widened the debate still further.

'Fair enough. Then there's a problem of the vanishing Mrs Mitchell. Is she already out of the country and he's joining her or is it even possible that she's gone the way of Harvey?'

'If you can do one, why not two?'

Emma listened as Kerr and Jacobson leap-frogged each other's speculations.

Eventually, if diffidently, she brought them back to the point.

'I'm still not convinced that her alibi *is* rock-solid. I'd like to do some checking this afternoon.'

Both Kerr and Jacobson saw this as a good idea but Kerr was less enthusiastic about Jacobson's parallel suggestion that he – Kerr – should look into the alleged weekend where-abouts of the Kents.

'Agreed it's something that needs doing as standard procedure but if you'd seen the state she was in this morning – you can't seriously think they're suspects in any real sense, surely?'

Jacobson had finally caught the evasive attention of Mr Behar's younger son. He ordered himself a second Kingfisher before he replied.

'Ian, Ian. You always need to look most closely at the closest, it's fundamental, basic.'

'I know but—'

'And hasn't it struck you that Roger Harvey with his brains bashed in was probably still a handsome bastard in comparison to Dr Kent? As for Mrs Kent – although of course I'm only going on your descriptions.'

Emma renewed her interest in the remains of the raita. Kerr felt sure his face must be reddening. He considered putting the obvious case against Jacobson's implied theory. The letters they'd taken away from Harvey's flat had spanned most of the last ten years and while they were nearly all from amorously enthralled women, Mrs Kent, like Laura Gregory, hadn't figured in the collection. He ate a forkful of rice and decided not to argue. For one thing he could do with getting out of Crowby for the afternoon. For another he knew that his objection was only valid up to a point anyway: after all both women had lived locally.

Jacobson tore off a slice of nan bread and changed the conversation to the virtues of Behar's lime pickle.

'The great thing is they make it here themselves. That's what makes the difference.'

*

David Mitchell looked like any other affluent sightseer on Warmoesstraat. Konica across his shoulder, Rohan trousers, soft leather shoes. It was unlikely too that he was the only one of the city's visitors whose walk looked steadier than it felt, whose temporarily poisoned system was calling out for a further assault.

A pigeon peck-peck-pecked in front of him and a suddenly revving car engine dinned in his brain. He turned up a side street and found himself right outside the place. De Bilderdijk – yes, this was it. An old man, stooped in an ancient grey coat, shuffled right past the entrance. He could do nothing but wait impatiently till he'd passed. Inside, the bar was a short room, two-tiered. It was crowded, noisy, but he recognized Kolb straightaway at the table opposite the end of the bar, just before the stairs up, to the left of the large, pulsating screen.

Big and solidly built, both fair-haired, they could have been brothers or well-matched, like-minded business partners. You reflect my success, I'll reflect yours. They shot shit for a good half-hour on either side of the matter. The Hamburg Trade Fair, opportunities in Eastern Europe, the future of electronic commerce. It was neither the most riveting nor the most irritating conversation on offer. Two ladies in PVC stopped in for a pre-shift heartwarmer. A loud American had loud and ill-informed views about the Middle East but even the loudest voices had to swim against Michael

Bolton, Tina Turner: the bland international currency of the video jukebox.

'Delay was inevitable but everything is checked out now, goot. It's all here. Bank accounts, all the necessary documents. You are a good programmer, Mr Mitchell.'

Mitchell was on his second beer, the world was relaxing again.

'It's a business transaction. That's how I see it. I do the work so why should the big guy cream the profits?'

Kolb was used to one-timers. For one thing, the single-hit-then-retire brigade cost less than the seasoned campaigners. A broad hand patted Mitchell's back. Kolb gave a complete service, he was up for a little nurse-maiding.

'Property *is* theft, Mr Mitchell, and capital will always seek the surplus value in labour. You don't need to justify yourself. Any man with spirit is a brigand.'

The taller of the PVC girls had a mane of red hair, swept back. In her boss's glossy catalogue, it was described as fiery. The American was insisting on buying her a drink. There was whisky and sausage on his breath. She pouted gracefully till it arrived, sent it back for more ice. Then she was off her stool, handbag over her arm.

'Here's mud in your eye, Texas!'

Nimbly, she pulled out his waistband, emptied the glass straight down inside. Even Mitchell could see it was the ideal moment to leave.

The final stretch of the Crow and Northern Canal had fallen into neglect and it was no longer possible to navigate the intersection with the Crow itself and come all the way into Crowby by water.

The grain store buildings behind Mill Street where the barges had once loaded up were now home to an intermittent Arts Centre which opened, thrived, lost its funding, closed and reopened at the untender mercy of the Leisure and Recreation Committee. An hour's backroads drive south brought you to Castlefoot lock where the Crow and Northern connected up to the bigscale waterway network. Downstream from the lock, the Castlefoot basin hadn't precisely thrived but had at least stayed open: only the most pessimistic assessor would have talked in terms other than steady growth, sustainable investment.

Kerr rounded the corner slowly, preparing for the sharp turn-off just past the hump-back bridge which spanned the canal as it ran into the basin. The Waterway Holiday Centre had grown up next to the Castle Arms and shared its car park. Kerr drew up close to the pub entrance but made his way first of all to the canal side; the canal shop opened for an hour a day in the quiet season and would be closing soon.

To his left, the holiday boats were drawn up en masse. Hardly any were on hire at this time of year. Across the water, the visitors' moorings were deserted. He rested his hand on the ancient but brightly and recently repainted diesel pump. Apply At Shop For Assistance: the sign was Sellotaped across the delivery gauge, handwritten but neat. Leaning out and squinting through the bridge in the weakening sunlight, he could see the private moorings where around a dozen narrowboats nestled against the coming weather under tarpaulin. A flotilla of ducks crested by, cutting a v shape in the water, disturbing a log, a half-submerged, rusting Coke can.

Kerr took in the shop's interior. Waterways books and maps, bread, baked beans, batteries – staples and basics in one corner and the rest given over to holidaymakers' tat. The magazine rack puzzled him for a moment before he realised why. It looked much the same as any given corner shop's until you sussed that the top shelf, normally the shrinkwrapped domain of *Busty* and *Leather Mistress*, had been entirely given over to titles like *True Crime, Great Unsolved Crimes* and even *Meet the Serial Killers*. Charming or what? Not that the selection seemed to have many takers. A good third of the covers had a faded, almost pre-decimal look.

A portly figure in a blazer, sandals and what his father would have called flannels was stocking up the shelf of 'Local Honey'. Kerr introduced himself, the nature of his visit.

'Albert Peck at your service, Detective Sergeant.'

Peck was tall when he unstooped himself, his handshake unconsciously strong. Kerr made him sixty, still athletic, his flab as superficial as the old-world, nautical manner. A risky business, the holiday industry. You wake up one day and you've actually turned into Mr Pickwick, the Yeoman of Old England or whatever.

'Mr and Mrs Kent though. I'm surprised to hear their fair name mixed up with the police.'

Captain bloody Birdseye in this case.

'It's purely routine, Mr Peck. There's no need to jump to conclusions.'

'I dare say, Detective Sergeant, mum's the word.'

Peck crossed the room, fumbled in a drawer next to the till. Kerr feared a pipe or Capstan Full Strength, if you still got them.

'You'll allow me my surviving vices, I hope. I can see you don't yourself, a wise man.'

'Please – go ahead.'

Kerr meant his reply in both senses. He was almost relieved to see the Benson and Hedges packet – a touch of reality, a hint of the actor out of role.

'A delightful couple, delightful. Moored here regularly for three years now and a shipshape craft too. Mr Kent's quite an authority on the history of the canals you know. We stock his book here though it's a bit on the intellectual side for most folks, Albert Peck included. He's not a bit stuffy though. He'll stand a round in the public bar when duty demands.'

Now that Peck mentioned it, Kerr could see half a dozen copies of John Kent's book amongst the other waterway books.

'Mrs Kent?'

'Fragrant is I believe the term in legal circles. A rose by any other name.'

Kerr turned a revolving postcard rack slowly, concealing his irritation.

'We're told they took their boat out last weekend.'

'I saw them arrive myself on Friday afternoon. About four o'clock, just after I'd shut up here. They hauled anchor on Saturday morning and I saw them getting back around seven on Sunday evening. Ten on Monday morning, they were putting her back under wraps.'

'You sound very definite, Mr Peck.'

'It's my job and my pleasure to keep a sharp eye on the basin. I'm here all the time too. *Pride of Manchester*, first through the bridge, that's my billet.'

Kerr made his escape as quickly as he could. Next to the door a red cardboard display asked Who's Who On The Canal? and offered plastic badges for a variety of personalities: Dogsbody, Gatecrasher, Admiral, Deckscrubber. Murder Suspect, he noticed, didn't seem to be in stock.

He crossed a patchy lawn to the Castle Arms

where a solitary, middle-aged barmaid was ringing the bell for last orders. The pub comprised a lounge and a saloon both served by the same central bar. He saw straightaway why the place wasn't staying open all afternoon: if she'd wanted to, she could have saved her arm and whispered the news to her total of three customers. Customer One passed Kerr in the doorway. He looked like a genuine enough old countryman but it was always possible he was another member of Captain Birdseye's Living Nostalgia troupe. Two and Three were a smartly dressed businessman and woman or a well-turned-out adulterous affair. They sat in a far corner, nursing their drinks, mutually absorbed. Business or pleasure: it seemed to be working for them, whichever it was.

The barmaid certainly knew the Kents.

'So does Ted. That's my husband, the licensee. They're the last people I'd expect you lot to come looking for. It's a respectable crowd we get in here.'

'I'm sure you're right. No question—'

He tried a smile that could still look boyish.

'A tomato juice with Worcestershire sauce would go down well.'

Look at me, Mrs, I'm a human being. I feel the cold on a day like this. I'm some mother's son.

'Yeah, well just so you know.'

The selling or screwing couple were leaving.

The man put their empty glasses on the bar. Not just a barmaid, the landlady. She beamed professionally, put Kerr's drink in front of him.

'Thank you so much for calling. Safe journey to you.'

It took him ten minutes to get her corroboration that the Kents had 'definitely' been in on Sunday evening. 'Old Albert' Peck had buttonholed Kent at the bar so she thought they'd left about ten.

'I expect they'd have stopped till closing if it hadn't been for that old pest. Once he's had four or five there's no shutting him up. It's all in his head as well. A life assurance salesman in Bradford. Never clapped eyes on a narrowboat before he came here.'

Kerr insisted on paying for the tomato juice, repeated that it was all routine, thanked her for her help.

'Well just so as you know, it's a respectable crowd we get in here.'

Back outside, Peck was locking up the shop front, checking and re-checking each padlock on the shutters like the crown jewels or a labful of illegal substances were boxed up inside. Maybe all the true crime magazines had turned the old boy paranoid or maybe it was the other way around and he stocked them to feed a pre-existing mania. Kerr took an avoidance route across the car park. Reaching the side of the bridge, he vaulted the padlocked red metal gate and took the winding steps down to the private moorings. The twisting railing would be largely obscured by high-growing gunera and hawthorn in summertime. Now, unencumbered by vegetation, the need for a paint job was all too apparent. Maybe it was one of the items on Birdseye's winter jobsheet.

Even if Peck hadn't told him and he hadn't already met Beatrice, he'd been around the Kents enough to know in any case that – amongst the *Flowers of Avon* and *Aphrodites – Sidney Webb* could only belong to them. He wondered whether the dog or the boat had been christened first. In his father's version of the history of socialism, there was room for only two sides: the heroes and the villains. He couldn't remember where he'd put the Webbs but he was sure they were in there somewhere.

There wasn't much to see from the exterior of the tarpaulin. Jacobson's hunch – if it was even really as strong as a hunch – wouldn't get them a warrant on its own and he wasn't about to risk a break-in with Peck in the vicinity. Across the water, half a dozen cows were lying down dozily at the end of a flat field, unaware that they'd taken up residence on the site of the long-vanished castle. Kerr regarded them gloomily. He was forced to concede that Jacobson had touched on something which was just about within the realms of the physically possible. An hour's drive, forty minutes if you pushed it; there was plenty of time after ten on Sunday to get to Crowby and back. *Sidney Webb* was the *Pride of Manchester*'s neighbour but Peck probably slept like a hibernating bear when he got back from the Castle Arms. It was a risk, but only a slight one, that someone would see or hear you starting the car engine or sneaking back in the early hours.

Kerr turned back towards the steps. The only problem for Jacobson's lunchtime theory – and Kerr still wasn't sure how seriously he'd meant it – was that there still wasn't the slightest shred of evidence or motive.

Jacobson gazed out of his office window and realized that the second pint of Kingfisher had been a mistake. The gulab jamal was another thing his digestive system could have lived quite happily without. All his body wanted him to do now was to find a quiet spot, put his feet up and doze out for the afternoon. Instead he took his emergency wake-up kit – towel, toothbrush, electric razor – to the Gents and stuck his face under the cold tap. Ten minutes later he forced down an unspeakably foul coffee in the police canteen and then drove over to Pelican House for his appointment with Eschaton Systems. In a country where large sections of the population never talked to their neighbours unless a national icon was dead or dying, workmates were a prime source of personal information.

Tony Davies set him up with a conference

room on the twelfth floor: fresh-cut flowers, jugs of iced water and freshly squeezed orange juice. No sign of a bloody ashtray, of course, but at least, Jacobson thought, the juice would kill the lingering memory of the coffee. He sat down at a mahogany table the size of the Amazon and Davies ushered in the three employees who'd worked most closely with David Mitchell. Two men and a woman: Sanjit Patel, Brian Kennedy, Judy Keegan. All three of them looked in their late twenties. He wanted a newer word than yuppie to stereotype them with but couldn't find one to hand. In the lift, Davies had called them the DawnTrader development team: 'Capital D, capital T, Inspector.' Mitchell had been their boss temporarily – what Davies called the senior developer – because the previous guy had been poached by a rival company. 'Something of a worry, Inspector. You make your staff sign confidentiality clauses obviously – but you can't take the inside knowledge they've picked up back out of their heads when they decide to leave.' Jacobson had thought selective lobotomy could be one obvious solution but he hadn't passed the suggestion on.

He poured himself out a full glass of orange juice, asked them if they could explain in layman's terms exactly what they did for a living. Patel and Kennedy deferred to Judy Keegan who, according to Davies, had stepped into Mitchell's role for the time being.

'We're what's known as an applications development team. Put simply, we write computer programs.'

'And the DawnTrader project, capital D, capital T?'

Tony Davies was leaving the room and she looked hesitantly towards him.

'It's OK, Judy, I think we can trust the police if no one else.'

Jacobson took a deep mouthful of orange juice and waited for her to continue.

'Oh right. Fine then. Well DawnTrader is basically a piece of software that makes predictions about stock market movements.'

Davies closed the door behind him and Judy Keegan seemed to relax a little. There was even the hint of a smile on her face.

'It's actually quite interesting—'

Jacobson lied as sincerely as he could, told her he was sure it was.

'Partly we've just brought together in one place a lot of tools that are already available separately. For instance when it's up and running, DawnTrader links online to the Internet so that it's always working with the latest available share prices and forecasts. But where we've really made some innovations is in the inference engine—'

Jacobson had to shake his head at this point. Patel cut in with a cogent summary.

'It's simple really. An inference engine is just

112

basically all the rules, best guesses and second guesses that human experts use when they need to reach a decision. The inference engine makes the computer an expert too: only one that works incredibly fast and never ever takes a day off.'

Judy Keegan ran her fingers through her shining auburn hair like a model in a shampoo ad and then carried on sounding like Einstein.

'Thanks, Sanjit. The thing about DawnTrader is that the inference engine is much bigger and much more sophisticated than anything that's been done before. Yet it's lean on memory too: the whole package will run on an ordinary personal computer. Literally anyone who wants to will be able to play the stock markets from home in real time.'

Jacobson followed maybe about fifty per cent of what had been said. But it was enough to grasp the money-making potential of what Eschaton was up to. No wonder Davies had a thing about confidentiality. He finished off his juice and asked them their feelings about David Mitchell.

Kennedy spoke for the first time.

'Great bloke. Just about the best programmer I've ever seen. Quite honestly we were weeks behind schedule before he came on board and now we're through to the final testing stage.'

Patel nodded in enthusiastic agreement.

'Contractors can be a bit funny sometimes. Not just that they get paid over the odds – they also want to keep their skills to themselves. But

Dave's been really helpful – gave me a whole load of tips I've never seen in the textbooks. I don't know why he wanted to go on a course though. He could probably teach *them*.'

'Believe it,' said Kennedy. 'He's a sociable guy too. A couple of times I've gone down the pub with him after work supposedly just for one and ended up there till shutting time.'

Jacobson asked him what topics of conversation Mitchell had over a drink.

Kennedy shrugged: 'Cars, soccer, the usual stuff. Women.'

'His wife?'

'Well, no, not really. But you don't down the pub, do you? He went back to Coventry every weekend though, didn't he Sanjit?'

Patel nodded again. But not last weekend, thought Jacobson.

'Did his wife ever call him at work then?'

All three of them shook their heads.

'The company policy is against personal calls anyway,' Patel volunteered, 'unless in an emergency.'

'When did you last have a drink with him, Mr Kennedy?'

'We had a few beers Wednesday of last week.'

'And he never mentioned that his wife was no longer living in the family home?'

Kennedy was incredulous but emphatic.

'What? No, he didn't – although like I say, he never talked much about her in the first place.'

'Did any of you ever hear him mention Roger Harvey?'

Patel and Kennedy looked doubtfully at each other but said nothing. It was left to Judy Keegan to break the silence.

'He only spoke about him once that I can think of. They seemed to have struck up a friendship because they were both interested in running. Dave used to run at least once a day or so he said. Anyway he thought I might know him because I was a student at Crowby. I didn't, of course. The computing faculty's not even on the same campus as all those grungy arts students.'

Jacobson signalled that the interview was over. For the most part, *Dave* Mitchell, as they were matily calling him, was shaping up like Norman Normal; a fact which told you nothing either way about his propensity for murder. Patel and Kennedy, mindful perhaps of some company rubric about the treatment of guests, shook his hand warmly in turn before they left the room. Judy Keegan stayed where she was until they'd both gone.

'There's another side to Dave Mitchell,' she said unprompted.

Jacobson sat back down again. She poured herself a glass of water and cleared her throat.

'He's brilliant at his work no question. Good-looking too *and* superficially charming. The kind that thinks they're god's gift, right? I made it totally clear I wasn't interested but he didn't let a little thing like that put him off. I'd look up from my work and he'd be quietly leering at me. He actually grabbed me one night when there were only the two of us working in the office. He said he knew I wanted it, all that fucking nonsense. Luckily, a cleaner came in.'

Jacobson asked if she'd reported the incident.

'I'm after a long-term career in this company, Inspector. Dave Mitchell will be gone – or would've been gone – when the project's complete. Whatever the directors say to your face or in public, no one really wants a woman who makes that kind of allegation around: and certainly not at a senior level. The fact that the cleaner saw what was happening got Mitchell off my case – so end of story.'

'Why tell me then, Judy?'

He watched her do the trick with her hair again before she answered. Sex in the workplace was a minefield or so he'd read.

'Because of what you're looking into. Somebody's murder. I don't mean that because he's a sexual harasser – or worse – he must be a murderer too. Obviously. It was just something about the look on his face when he heard the cleaner at the door and realized he'd have to let me go. I'm talking about a few seconds really. But it was such total anger, such total hatred. It just made me think he was capable of anything – anything at all.'

*

The tired-looking young woman from the night before turned out to be called Maureen. Somehow, they'd never met on her previous visits to the Refuge. She was still looking tired as she showed Emma Smith back into the same makeshift office.

On the bay window, the thick hessian curtains which shielded the interior after dark had been drawn back. Fading daylight filtered through net curtains which were always protectively in place. To the side of the window, a steaming kettle sat on the draining board of a small metal sink. She followed the steam trail across the poster of the cartoon girl jumping with joy and empowerment. 'Never Give Up!' said the crayony writing. There would be instant coffee this time. Things sometimes got better.

'Laura's not here. She's at a meeting with the Social Services. Probably won't get back till around five.'

'So there's only the two of you work here full-time?'

'That's the official picture, anyway. Some of our volunteers put more energy in here than they do in their paid jobs. I actually live here though. Came here to get away from a bastard. When I'd got myself together, I found I seemed to be some use at talking other women through it all – so now I'm a live-in counsellor.'

'And Laura?'

'Coordinator, administrator, inspiration – you

name it. It's her enthusiasm that keeps us going when it all gets too heavy and, believe me, it often does.'

'She sleeps over here sometimes?'

'About three times a week on average. I do two nights on call as well and we've a rota of volunteers for the other nights. It's a big task here to rebuild self-esteem, convince a woman she can run her own life. In the early days at least it's reassuring to have what looks like a more-or-less professional presence permanently available.'

'She was here on Sunday night, we're told.'

'Sunday and Mon—'

Maureen had made two cups, was about to hand one to her visitor.

'Look, what is this? Laura's not accused of any crime. What gives you the right to—'

Emma took the cup anyway.

'I understand how you feel, Maureen, but this is a murder inquiry. We have to ask awkward questions, raise doubts about worthwhile citizens. The bottom line is if we can't get information voluntarily, we can compel it. Assisting the police with their inquiries. I'm sure you've heard the phrase.'

Maureen moved over to the imposing desk in the middle of the room. Stripped pine, green varnish; a donation from the Wood Women's Collective. She knew it was a bluff, yet knew too that if it came to it, they could get a warrant, harass every resident. Laura had been here anyway so there was no real problem,

'So macho! I expect you even carry handcuffs.'

She tried not to let her face flush, managed to stay silent. I'm only doing my job, I'm only doing my job: the police mantra. She clasped the warmth of the coffee mug, watched Maureen produce an old-fashioned office register.

'We keep a full record of night cover. Time in, time out, contact with residents, significant incidents.'

Emma studied the entry for Sunday evening. Laura Gregory had taken over at ten pm, had been relieved at seven am. She'd counselled a Mrs Wilkinson at midnight and, at two am, she'd phoned Crowby Central with regard to a possible prowling husband. According to the register, there'd been a police response at two twenty am.

'Is Mrs Wilkinson here just now?'

'Christ, you're really serious about this aren't you? I'll need to check, if you'll give me a minute.'

Maureen left the room and Emma waited. The taste in her mouth wasn't just coffee.

Jackie Wilkinson turned out to be barely nineteen. Herself, her babies and all her worldly goods were crammed into an attic room. A slanted window on the angled roof cast fading daylight on to the table where she was padding the shoulders of a black velvet jacket. Her hair was long, fair, straight. She wore a flowing, loose-fitting dress. Someone much older than Emma might have looked at her and been reminded of good vibes, love beads, the strange days of gentler times. Near her feet, her twin sons were sleeping peacefully in their cots. It was obvious she wasn't keen on talking to police but her story tallied exactly with the night duty register.

'I just couldn't get to sleep at all. My sister told me on Saturday that Joe's been following her in the street, threatening her for my address. It was on my mind all weekend. Laura made me coffee, listened to me till I felt a bit calmer, more able to cope. It was after one when I went back to bed. I don't know how she does it – she's so patient, so reassuring.'

Maureen followed her frostily downstairs and opened the front door with impressive silence. Driving back to the Divi, Emma recalled her conversation with Marilyn Wright and DS Kerr's description of the Wynarth Arms incident. Murder wasn't an either/or matter: Inspector Jacobson's words. Neither it seemed was Laura Gregory.

Jacobson removed his jacket and hung it precariously on the bending wooden coat rack Janice had intended for the skip when they'd made their last house-move together. Jacobson had rescued it as a homely touch for his office but now the stem had come away from the base and it supported itself and any hanging garments only if it was positioned carefully against the wall. He tucked the hefty wad of documents under his chin to get his jacket off and nearly dropped them in the process. He'd only asked for the last month's data but some zealous bastard at the credit card centre had faxed through every transaction going back two years. The police, he'd long since realised, didn't have a monopoly on instinctual authoritarianism. An unpleasant mindgame he'd sometimes played was to wonder how the last century would have turned out if the Third Reich had lasted into the era of Microsoft.

He clicked on his desk lamp and sat down with Harvey's credit card statements. The Open Team Approach was the current buzzword amongst the senior management of the force. It meant amongst other things that he should be spending more time in the incident room. He separated the last pages from the rest and swung his feet comfortably across the desk. Jacobson knew at least two things they didn't seem to grasp upstairs. One: a team works better without constant supervision. Two: by this stage in the day, he needed to be able to hear himself think.

It was immediately clear that Harvey had pulled his weight as a consumer. The lifestyle of a relatively affluent bachelor was confirmed by record shops, wine stores, restaurants, theatre tickets. Jacobson came to the page which had been generated by the last week of the dead man's life. His last credit card purchase had been on Saturday afternoon, 15:16:07 – a trip to Waitrose. The Egyptians, who liked to stock up for the good times ahead in the afterlife, would probably have approved, but his own favourites, the Sumerians, had mostly taken a grimmer, less optimistic view of mortality. According to *The Epic of Gilgamesh*, over the bolt and door of the house of the dead lay silence while in the darkness inside there was only dust and clay to be eaten. He started to feel the onset of a yawn perpetrated by his own still heftily full stomach as he looked back through the rest of Saturday and Friday. But the yawn vanished when he turned to the details for Thursday evening. His feet came off the desk and his brain raced mileages, distances.

Harvey had filled up on the way out of Wynarth at nine fifty-five pm, Thursday night, which fitted in with him leaving the Kents at around a quarter to ten. He'd called in for petrol again on Friday afternoon. Except that this time he'd picked up the tokens towards his free tumbler on the shores of Lake Windermere. It didn't really look like the action of a man who'd told his friends he wanted an early night.

Before he'd paid the ferryman, Dr Roger Harvey had made a final earthbound journey to a destination he'd wanted to keep to himself.

*

Kerr called in on the Kents again. Annie Kent's eyes were still red but now her hair had been combed. She was still on cigarettes but there didn't seem to be any gin this time. He needed to re-check their version of the weekend now that he'd spoken to Albert Peck and the Castle Arms' landlady. He needed to know more about their friendship with Roger Harvey. He needed to make arrangements for them to check the contents of Harvey's flat and ensure that the police examination hadn't missed the evidence of some subtle theft or other. Christ: he was in the middle of a murder investigation – it definitely wasn't that he just wanted to see her again.

'John's driven over to the funeral director's. I don't think he'll be long.'

Kerr sat in her kitchen, the same chair as the day before. He tasted the tea in the same Oxfam mug. Too hot. Like yesterday, like earlier today, he was still seeing the eyes, the face, the body before he heard the voice – still hearing the voice before he took in the words. He blew on the surface, took another sip.

'You've said Dr Harvey was a regular visitor. The games of squash, meals, visits down the pub. Did he ever return the compliment?'

'He's not – he wasn't – much of a cook if that's what you mean. Lived out of the microwave as far as I know. I don't think he entertained much at home, except for his girlfriends of course.'

123

'So you and your husband never visited his flat?'

He'd put the question in a standardly devious way. He was doing his job properly. It didn't matter to him, couldn't matter, whether she gave the right answer or not.

'Not to eat anyway but we do – did – go round there. Roger's estate is next to the superstore and the multiplex cinema. So sometimes we'd call in if we were late-night shopping or if there was a decent film on.'

Mrs Kent's attempt at a smile suggested that the latter was an infrequent occurrence. Class, status, taste, education: even in trauma, there were appearances to keep up.

'So when were you last there?'

'It was a week ago on Tuesday. They were showing *Forget Venice* again for one night only. He gave us a glass of wine but he seemed keen to get back to his word processor. John asked him if he wanted to come with us but he said he wanted to work on so we left him to it.'

Kerr's memory replayed in sequence the old film programme in Harvey's kitchen drawer, the sight of Chief Inspector Jacobson on his knees with the piles of videos.

'We'd got the impression that he was a bit of a film buff himself.'

'He was – much more so than me or John. He even gave a series of talks at the Film Theatre a couple of years ago. It was when they had a season on Spain in the thirties.'

Kerr tried the tea again. Annie took out another cigarette. He told her about the fingerprint cross-check, wondered if she'd work out later how underhand – how *police* – that made his question about their visits to Harvey's flat.

'Oh yes, I see. It was when it was finally confirmed that we couldn't have children. I just fell to pieces for a while. Shoplifting! The lonely housewife's cry for help. Getting caught helped me to confront reality, I think. It all seems a long time ago now. We're brought up to accept only certain states as normal – motherhood, marriage.'

She looked across at him and again he saw the face before he heard the words.

'In the end you come to realize that you have to live your life in your own way.'

He always carried a lighter as well as the professional pack of cigarettes. He leant across the table and she steadied her fingers on his hand as she took the light.

I know exactly what you mean! The words had left his brain, had almost got to his lips when the front door opened and the slumbering Beatrice Webb woke up, barked at John Kent's return. He might have told her about Cathy, how people change, drift apart. They might have talked for hours, maybe not just talked. But the possibility of one afternoon had faded irreversibly into the definiteness of another. Into this one. The one where the husband came back and the sky outside was an unswerving grey.

Chapter Five

Jacobson decided he'd better see what was happening in the incident room. When he got there, DC Barber was taking his stint at fielding the Looney Tunes callers while DCs Williams and Mick Hume were sifting dispiritedly through the mounting pile of unhelpful interview statements taken from Harvey's heard-nothing, seen-nothing neighbours. Kerr and Emma Smith were drinking tea and comparing notes on Laura Gregory and the Kents. As Jacobson passed the fax machine, it stuttered suddenly into life. The fax that came through was from British Telecom. Unlike the unknown zealot at the credit card centre, he saw that at least BT's operative had only supplied them with precisely what they'd asked for: a record of the calls on Harvey's number in the past two months. Jacobson took a sheet of numbers himself, divided the remainder out equally to the rest of the team.

The first call he examined deepened the

connection to David Mitchell. Late on a Monday night, nearly six weeks before he'd been killed, Harvey had talked for ten minutes to Mitchell's Coventry address. The timing of the call, Jacobson soon discovered, was exceptional. Harvey hadn't used his phone all that often, hadn't even bothered with an answerphone. He'd made a second Monday night call *chez* Mitchell a fortnight later but mostly he'd made occasional daytime calls to extensions at the university or to the home numbers of colleagues, including – unremarkably – John Kent. An international call to Los Angeles turned out to be work-related too: it seemed Harvey had been invited to present a conference paper at UCLA. There had been several calls to and from a number which had a Kendal dialling code but it was either wrong or incomplete. Given that Harvey – or at least his credit card – had been in the Lake District just two days before his murder, Jacobson made a note that BT would have to re-check it for them urgently, try and come up with the correct data.

The other numbers on the sheet all began with the code for Crowby. Part of the routine in these cases was to cross-reference against the Division's localized database of current and recent investigations. In theory, if a phone number or address was Known To The Police, then something would show up. Jacobson crossed off two calls to Kwik-Fit, three to the tandoori takeaway, one to Domino's Pizza. He keyed in the next number with dwindling enthusiasm. He'd been convinced from the start that Harvey's death had no professional criminal connection anyway. But only seconds later the details were before him on the screen: indisputable, flickering amber – a multiple occupancy address listed as under surveillance and complete with a drug squad case reference. As if that wasn't enough, the call itself had been made on Sunday night, the very eve of the murder. Shows how much I know, he thought.

The daylight was fading. Professor Merchant sat alone at his desk in his office near the mortuary. The room was quiet and his calls were on hold. There was no point trying to work on. His concentration was gone until he could resolve the issue, make up his mind. At first it had just seemed like natural curiosity on her part. He'd told her the likeliest time of death, the murderer's *modus operandi*: everything anyone could need to construct a solid, watertight alibi. It had only seemed like courtesy when she'd promised not to mention his very existence should the police question her about her relationship with Harvey. It shouldn't come to that anyway. She already had a genuine alibi in any case, hadn't she? She couldn't be in two places at once after all.

Every drawer in his desk had a separate lock. He unlocked the bottom drawer and took out a padlocked metal box. He unlocked that too and took out the folder which he'd long ago stamped as CONFIDENTIAL. His secret garden. Slowly, methodically, he worked his way through the pile of letters, photographs, hotel receipts, intimate mementoes.

The fifteen years of his second marriage equated to at least as many serious affairs. He'd almost lost count of the casual encounters – the one-night or two-week stands – and the flirtations to which he pleaded technically not guilty on the grounds of non-consummation. Elspeth suspected, he knew, but she'd never come close to real discovery. Intrigue, deception, concealment, he excelled at the clandestine just as he excelled in the other areas of his life.

God knows, he'd thought of leaving her, the children, their big, solid house often enough. Never for another woman but for himself – to be free! Yet he'd realised each time that what he actually wanted, claimed for himself, was all of it, both sides, everything. He needed the constancy of the elegant, faithful, intelligent, cheated wife every bit as much as the shifting, changing panorama of the women he termed his mistresses. The elaborate complexity of his deceit was as integral to his pleasure as the women themselves.

Finally, he came to the one picture of Laura Gregory which he'd kept. He noticed it had become creased on the top right corner. There were probably as many reasons for adultery as there were adulterers but Merchant felt he understood his own case well enough: it was one of the games of dark satisfaction left open to you when you stared out at the world through intelligent eyes and found it empty of purpose, random, meaningless.

The waiter had taken the photograph for them. It had been that night at the Rome conference when Calvino had driven them out to the restaurant in the hills. It was good too. You could make out the trees round the terrace with their strings of coloured lightbulbs, read the label on the valpolicella, the details of her smile. A man of hidden talents evidently. He recalled the sensation of her knee rubbing against his leg and then her hand following as he'd steered the talk away from methodologies, new instrumentation and on to God, the Italian's re-kindled Catholicism, his universal vision. A year later he'd been dead from a swift, sudden cancer. Even the mortician, he thought, hits the slab in the end.

He was having to strain to see but he still didn't bother with the light switch. Her face wore an urgent smile, a smile which, when he thought about it now, seemed almost hysterical. There was no getting away from it: *she might have done it!* The thought was loud in his mind, like an ugly, persistent voice. He knew he'd only kept her on so well beyond her sell-by date in pure fear: any abandonment would have catapulted her straight to Elspeth. He'd practically twisted Harvey's arm into it when he'd noticed her obvious interest in him. Inviting both of them to the Michael Nyman concert – even implying that Nyman had been an old university acquaintance – and then dropping out himself 'under pressure of work' at the last minute had been his master-stroke. All in all, Harvey had provided a neat solution to the Laura Gregory problem until his murder boosted Crowby's serious crime rate. Now a local difficulty had gone global, nuclear: the careful architecture of his dazzling double-life would crumble in the construction of any halfway competent prosecutor's case. 'How did you come to meet Roger Harvey, Ms Gregory? I see. So you had also previously been having a sexual relationship with Professor Merchant?'

It took all of his ingrained, polished reflexes not to swear at his secretary when she appeared in the doorway, itemized the number of outstanding calls.

'Fine, Doreen, fine. Just give me five minutes.'

Merchant put the photo back in the folder and put the folder back in the box. *She really might have done it*!

Hayle Close persisted at the furthest end of Mill Street. Kerr turned the corner slowly, taking in the latest spray-painted message across the corrugated metal defences of Hudson's scrapyard, a bright blue scrawl: DRUGS NOT JOBS. The row of terraced houses next door ended abruptly at number thirty-two. After that came the broad stretch of wasteland which bordered the sodium-lit roar of the inner ring road. Half the properties were boarded up but they weren't necessarily empty. Number twenty-four itself turned out to be one of the few which were still legally rented. Kerr pulled the unfamiliar vehicle awkwardly to a halt. They were using a customized VW camper van for the operation, the windows tinted black, the side panels bright yellow where they weren't green polka-dot. It was one of the drug squad's special vehicles: blend in by standing out. He switched off the engine and looked out watchfully, trying to size up the situation. Emma Smith slid open the passenger door and got out.

Beyond an upstairs window, a bare light bulb hung on a curling wire from a ceiling which had been amateurishly glossed in cheap brown paint. If this was Mr Big's place, he didn't want to see Mr Smallfry's gaff. According to the drug squad of course, the guy *was* big – a sub-agent not a street-level dealer – and their operation – as always – had reached a crucial stage. Jacobson hadn't been able to swing it alone. Detective Chief Superintendent Chivers had needed to pull the strings before they'd grudgingly agreed to let DC Smith go in low-key as the grieving relative, supposedly working her way through the deceased's address book. Even then they'd insisted on a drug squad vehicle and on the presence of a drug squad officer: both to be charged over the odds to Jacobson's budget.

She seemed to be getting past the front door easily enough. Kerr was genuinely impressed. Even allowing for the drug squad's notorious over-exaggeration, it still took nerve to carry off this particular game of soldiers. The VW came complete with a box of appropriate music tapes. He shoved on Trance Dance Explosion and checked his watch. She'd been gone less than three minutes. They'd agreed fifteen as the cut-off but now he wondered if that was too long. He glanced at Harry Fields, sitting glumly in the back seat. The drug squad's reluctant representative looked straight through him. In point of fact, he hadn't opened his mouth once since they'd left the Divi.

Emma was back on the street inside ten minutes. Kerr turned up the volume as she walked back towards the van. Still in role, she buried her face in her hands as they drove off.

'I'm sorry but it looks like a blind alley. The call was nothing to do with the drugs suspect at all. He's got his younger brother and his girl-friend staying with him. A decent enough kid by the looks of it. Scrapes a living teaching Tai Chi, would you believe? It seems Harvey was interested in joining one of his classes, apparently told him he was feeling a bit stressed out.'

Kerr jerked the gear stick. He was getting used to disappointment on this case.

'I'll believe it. You didn't happen to find out when the classes are? Old Harry here looks like he could benefit from some relaxing exercise.'

Because of the Hayle Close operation the evening briefing was delayed until six o'clock. Superintendent Chivers had stayed around after the negotiations with the drug squad and he gave a personal update on the Interpol and national angles. Thanks to the house-search by Coventry CID, he told them, copies of the Mitchells' wedding photograph and stills from a recent holiday video would soon be with every major police station in Holland. The photos were also being circulated to the media. They'd missed the *Crimewatch* deadline but some of the regional crime programmes were expected to carry the story over the weekend. There was even an outside chance of front page coverage in the tabloids as long as there wasn't another pop star or politician caught in the wrong bed at the wrong time before morning. KLM and other relevant companies had been asked to list outward bookings made by British passport-holders since Monday: 'We can't assume that Holland is friend Mitchell's final destination. It could just be a stopping-off point.'

Jacobson grabbed a plate of sausages and chips in the police canteen after the briefing but salved his conscience by turning down the opportunity of a fried egg on the side. He'd listened closely to Chivers's gloss on the progress of the investigation. All in all the old boy had given the impression of being mildly pleased. The subtext, Jacobson thought, was easy enough to read. As the force's most senior detective, Chivers would be home and dry if the case against Mitchell could be shored up – regardless of whether he was ever caught. It wouldn't be Crowby's fault if the killer slipped through the hands of incompetent forces in another country and in official eyes Chivers would be seen to have made all the right moves. Once again, appearance would triumph over substance. It was how things went at the top management level. His own problem, he realized, was that he still actually cared about justice and bringing the guilty to book. He believed in what he saw as the true purpose of the job: it was a commitment which would probably keep him an inspector until the day he retired.

The vehicle workshop was in a separate building a couple of streets away. Jacobson set off on foot. He didn't want to get stuck in the tail-end of the rush-hour exodus to the suburbs and Marilyn's, his second destination, was over in that direction anyway. The workshop floor looked and smelt like any other big garage, the air thick with engine fumes. Only the serried ranks of white patrol cars marked it out as a police location. He walked carefully around a hazardous-looking pool of oil and approached the thick screen of polythene which had been erected to shield off Roger Harvey's car and its forensic examiners.

Jacobson's expression was pure suffering. He only wanted to look in the glove compartment but the apparition – white lab coat, gloves, mouth mask – muttered on: body hairs, skin samples, fibres, Christ-knows-what human detritus.

'Ahbulaawuzorra.'

'What?'

The white glove moved across the face, the mask was removed.

'I'm sorry, Inspector. I said this was all we found in the way of contents.'

'What was?'

The unmasked scientist beckoned Jacobson over to a nearby workbench.

'A couple of petrol vouchers, a newspaper, an AA book and a road atlas. Kept his interior neat and tidy apparently. I'd say it had been vacuumed within the last week.'

Jacobson picked up the atlas.

'May I?'

'Be my guest, Inspector.'

The invitation was half-hearted at best; he made a big show of carefulness as he took the atlas out of the bag, started to thumb through the maps. The place names caught his eye like the pages in a kid's flicker-book. Edinburgh, Glasgow, Newcastle, Haltwhistle. Here's where we get off – Carlisle,

137

Cockermouth, the Old Man of Coniston ...
Windermere! He followed the road towards
Kendal and then the curve of the A6 as it crossed
Shap Fell. A minor road bent leftwards, leading
nowhere or, more precisely, towards an outcrop
of buildings which the mapper had designated as
Scarsbeck. It was an obscure detail on the page but
Jacobson's attention was drawn straight to it for
one simple reason: the word Scarsbeck was encir-
cled by a neatly drawn loop which had been
executed in thick black biro. He'd given the team
the night off on the basis that they'd be available
for the whole of the rest of the weekend if necessary but DC Barber had volunteered to do a
half-shift in the incident room until ten. He called
him up from his mobile on his way out.

'Chase BT up again, lad – and keep chasing
the sods. We need that Lake District number
yesterday.'

He'd offered to call on Matt Ramshaw at the
Film Theatre itself but Ramshaw had suggested
meeting across the way at Marilyn's. Since it
called itself a wine bar, Jacobson gambled and
lost on a glass of Australian Cabernet. He
looked along the counter to where a life-size
model replicated the famous billowing dress
scene from *The Seven Year Itch*. At last he
spotted Ramshaw at a corner table and edged
his way through the crowd. Ramshaw had sensi-
bly stuck to lager and had deposited a sliver of
lime in the ashtray. On the wall to their side,

138

the real Marilyn dragged on her cigarette and looked wistfully down on Manhattan from her balcony.

As far as culture was a feature of Crowby beyond tv and the video shop, Ramshaw deserved his share of credit or blame. He'd run the Film Theatre for several years now, still had his weekly jazz show on Crowby FM. Jacobson knew him only because an unfortunate set of circumstances had briefly made him a suspect in the Crawler case. Jacobson's thoroughness had cleared his name. More: Jacobson's discretion had kept his name from the press while the investigation proceeded. Unsurprisingly, Ramshaw had sounded keen to return the favour. Not that Jacobson had big hopes for their meeting. At this stage in the case he simply needed all the background he could get.

'Yes. I remember the Civil War season all right. "To Die In Madrid" we called it. Roger Harvey introduced a couple of the films and got the chance to plug his own book – the usual kind of thing. He turned in a pretty good performance as it turned out. He was knowledgeable but off-the-cuff at the same time. Went down pretty well.'

Ramshaw paused for a drink. He'd evidently smartened up his act since the last time Jacobson had seen him. The pony tail, designer stubble and Levis had been ditched for a smooth haircut and an expensive-looking suit.

'I think the last time I saw him was in this place actually. Must have been a year, maybe eighteen months ago. I remember it because I got caught up in this daft row with Laura Gregory. She's the woman who runs the refuge for—'

Jacobson's nod told him they already knew who she was.

'Anyway, I'd only called in for a quick one but she wanted to collar me for a bloody discussion about the difference between pornography and eroticism, starts telling me what was supposed to be wrong with half the films we were showing.'

A team of Marilyn wannabees, some more convincing than others, were distributing free night-club passes to appropriate tables. Jacobson and Ramshaw didn't seem to qualify although Jacobson suspected that Ramshaw might just have about made it if he'd been there on his own or in less antique company. He watched the nearest one slink past without the slightest glance in his direction.

'So she was here with Roger Harvey then?'

'Exactly. Harvey calmed her down, persuaded her not to actually pour flavoured vodka down the front of my shirt.'

Ramshaw grinned, took another gulp from his bottle.

'Old Ally, on the other hand, never said a bloody word.'

'Old Ally?'

'Yeah, Ally Merchant. Some kind of big cheese at the hospital. His wife is one of our major sponsors. I think he had an interest in the Gregory woman himself at one time. I even remember speculating whether there was some kind of threesome going on there.'

He took another, bigger gulp and put the bottle back down on the table with a thud.

'My fault if there was. I introduced Harvey to both of them on the first night of the Civil War season.'

The crowd had doubled, even trebled, by the time Jacobson got up to leave. A group of women were being particularly raucous on the other side of the room, wolf-whistling and harassing the waiters. One of them looked like Kerr's wife, Cathy, but it was difficult to tell in this light, at this distance. Near the exit, he narrowly avoided a collision with a Marilyn cut-out who was clasping a menu to her cleavage. A female bouncer held the door open for him with a practised, patronising smile. It was the oldest he'd felt all day.

Kerr pulled into the drive and switched off the engine. He sat in the car, staring at the garage door. He saw Annie Kent undressing for him, imagined the feel of her breasts, her body. A woman he'd only just met. But a woman who wasn't Cathy. A woman who was unfamiliar, new. He told himself he couldn't carry on like this any longer. Maybe he was too straight a copper for it to be Mrs Kent but that only meant it would happen with someone else. He thought about the first time he'd seen this house, the first night he'd slept in it with Cathy, the weeks they'd spent decorating it room by room, making love in turn on each newly carpeted floor. After a few minutes, he got out, walked towards the porch. It was as if somewhere in the ordinariness of their lives, amongst the shopping trips, the holidays, the tv programmes they watched together, something extraordinary had been choked to death.

He turned the key in the latch. It wasn't possible to wait. He'd tell her now, find a mate's sofa for the weekend. The cat brushed against his leg, meowing. He stroked her gently and entered the hall. He put down his case folder and resolutely opened the door to the lounge. He saw at once that she wasn't there, wasn't home. *Fuck!* He should have realized when her car hadn't been outside: since when had Cathy bothered with the garage? *Fuck!* There was a row of knick-knacks on top of the old pub piano he'd bought for her from the market in Wynarth. She'd always wanted a piano, she'd told him. But although he'd had the keys tuned, the wood stained and polished, she'd never bothered to learn. *Fuck!* He slammed his hand right along, sent them all crashing to the floor.

When he'd calmed down enough to trust himself in the kitchen, he went through and switched on the kettle. He flung a teabag into a chipped mug. It wasn't properly clean but it was the cleanest one he could find. By now there were two days' worth of dirty dishes next to the sink but neither he nor Cathy had been prepared to relent and wash up. When he'd made the cup of tea, he brought the case folder in from the hall, took out the photocopied set of Roger Harvey's letters. Not for the first time, he wondered what he'd do if he wasn't police, if he didn't have something bigger than himself to think about. Like the rest of the team, he'd already studied the letters to the point where he could almost recite them by heart. He knew that all he was doing was hiding in the job, burying himself inside it: but just knowing something didn't mean you stopped doing it.

Virtually all the letters that Harvey had wanted to keep were what used to be called love letters. Some were romantic, tender. Some were trivial, chatty. Some were sexually explicit. Many were all three. Yet there'd been nothing from Laura Gregory and only one letter from Harvey's supposedly most recent girlfriend, Melissa Woolstone – a short, friendly note which said little more than that she hoped Harvey's book was going well and that there was more going on in Wellington than she'd expected, particularly in the university area. The only two real surprises concerned the presence of a letter which Roger Harvey had written himself, apparently on the twenty-sixth of August. Firstly, it had a small black and white photograph pasted on the top left corner. Secondly, it had evidently never been posted.

Kerr picked it out and looked at it again. The photo was an interior shot of a young woman with long plaited hair sitting at a pub table. There was a glass of wine in front of her and she held a cigarette to her mouth through slender fingers. It was almost an advertising image, almost a cliché, but Kerr still felt the dark, oval eyes, straight-to-camera, pulling him in, grabbing his attention.

I'm looking at the photograph as I write. I can't sleep now, not tonight. Maybe you remember? You had half a dozen of them but this was the only one you'd let me have. Nigel Somebody had taken them the summer before we met, the summer my parents had their car crash. He must have reckoned he was Doisneau or something! We were so naïve then, weren't we? All of us really. You know, Alison, I really did believe that you were my one true and forever love in those days. After you'd gone, I honestly thought I couldn't go on living without you. I just used to sit in my room and gaze at this picture, sometimes for hours at a stretch. John (Kent – remember him?) used to call me young Werther! And

144

now, finally, after all these years, here you are on my doorstep again.

Jacobson got back home at half past eight laden with inquiry materials. Barber had promised to contact him as soon as BT came back with the correct Lake District phone number and he'd arranged with Sergeant Ince to have the Mitchells' holiday video sent over if it arrived at the Divi during the evening shift. The video was unlikely to contain anything vital but you could never be sure, should never overlook any detail. He glanced briefly at Harvey's collection of *billets-doux*, wondered again about the arty snap of the young woman in the bar. He found his copy of the press release package and spread out the stills from the video on the dining room table. At least he had these to be going on with – Mitchell, big, muscular, emerging from the sea and his wife, smiling, throwing him a beach towel. This woman was dark-haired too but thirty-something not twenty. In the last shot she was bare-breasted, the black bikini top discarded in the sand. Jesus! He really was in danger of turning into a dirty old man: licking his fat lips at pictures of girls in – or getting out of – swim-suits. He put the pictures back where they came from, decided it was time for a glass of whisky.

He'd dumped the post on the kitchen table when he'd got in. He looked at it again now. Bills, a yellow envelope offering high-quality prints and your next film free. At the bottom of the pile, a windowed enveloped proclaimed 'Frank and Janice Jacobson' above the address details. He poured the whisky before he opened it.

Dear valued customer,
 The Morricone family hopes to welcome you during the GALA WEEK of SPECIAL EVENTS to celebrate the opening of OUR NEWEST TRATTORIA under the Personal supervision of Paul Morricone, Jnr.'

It always had to be Italian or occasionally French with Janice. Mr Behar had never met his wife, not even when he'd had one. He was about to chuck this less than exclusive invitation into the bin when it occurred to him that it might be something special to do with Sally if their date came off. He carried his drink into the lounge, switched on the cd player. It was the matter of details again: he'd borrowed *Astral Weeks* from Kerr, hoping to fathom some possible element in the connection between Harvey and Mitchell. As far as he could see, all that the jargon of profiling really amounted to was the attempt to see the world through the suspect's eyes, the suspect's experiences.

Jacobson's bar-room line was that the great era of rock and roll had ended somewhere around the time of Chuck Berry's second extended gig in the state penitentiary. Privately, his tastes were a good deal wider although haphazardly formed. He'd heard of Van Morrison for years but this was the first time he'd knowingly listened to him. The music was better than he'd expected, different too. By the time he'd played as far as 'Cypress Avenue', he was thinking seriously about finally putting himself off-duty for the night. What did he really think the video was going to tell him anyway? Even if Barber did come back with the telephone number, what was he going to do with it before tomorrow? On his way to the kitchen for whisky number two, he turned up the volume control so that the music could follow him through.

Everything was done, arranged. There were three hours before the flight, two hours before the taxi would carry him across the city to Schiphol. David Mitchell showered, shaved, changed his trousers, selected a clean shirt.

Passport, tickets, bank account details, ready cash: he managed to squeeze each essential item into his wallet. Carefully, he re-checked the contents then – satisfied – shoved it deep into the left-hand inside pocket of his leather blouson, zipped the pocket tightly shut. It was a jacket Jean had never liked, had discouraged him from wearing. Well, it was none of her business now. There was nearly two hundred quid in Dutch notes and coins scattered on the bed. He picked them up, smoothed down the notes, stuffed them in the outside pocket, right-hand side. That way he wouldn't have to disturb his escape kit till he was safely at the airport.

He looked carefully around the hotel room. Both cases were packed, nothing had been left lying, everything was ready. Turning towards the door, he smiled to himself, patted his chest, felt the wallet nestling securely across his heart. He'd done it! He'd bloody well done it!

There'd been scarcely a flaw so far. Kolb's delays had cost him two days but he was still well within his time-frame. There was only the airport, the flight and the other airport to get through and he'd be free, smelling sweet. You could see from the quality of the documents that Kolb's team were professionals, winners. Kolb's advice had been sound too: just look relaxed, confident. By the time he'd finished his fourth beer in his third café it was pretty much how Mitchell felt anyway – almost as if he was genuinely and innocently on holiday. A tourist taking in the usual sights. He settled the bill, went out into Oude Hoogstraat.

On impulse, he crossed the pavement, peered through the doors of the Cloud Ten. The interior of the coffee shop was hi-tech, noisy. It reminded him of the bar where he'd met Kolb earlier in the day. Neither of these factors decided him against the idea, he just couldn't afford a fuddled brain at the airport. Mellow, yes. Stoned, no. That could come later. Anything at all he wanted could come later. What was important right now was to get back to the hotel on time.

He walked off in what he was sure was the direction of Damstraat. Probably it wasn't the quickest way but it was the route he felt he could picture best in his mind. After ten minutes, he conceded to himself that he was lost. The one street should have led seamlessly into the other. When that hadn't happened, he'd turned a couple of corners in quick succession. Now where the hell am I? He knew he was still somewhere in the Walletjes, the Red Light District, but the street was quiet; he was no longer on the standard tourist circuit. There was a bar, brown café style, just ahead. He decided to ask for directions there, even call a taxi if necessary.

He couldn't believe it at first. He was tall, broad-shouldered, capable – every bit as strong as he looked. He was surely the last type a street criminal would choose. The guy must be a clown or a masochist. It wasn't even dark enough for the shadows to hide his features. He was rat-faced, dirty: Dustin Hoffman in that old sixties movie about New York.

'Hand it over or I'll shoot your cock off.'

The voice was young and English. He sounded for all the world like an ex-public schoolboy.

'You must be joking, pal.'

The guy *had* to be a joker. He was actually poking his finger inside his coat pocket, pretending he had a gun! It would have been funny if he hadn't been in a hurry, hadn't had a new life to begin.

'Just get out my way, pal, and you won't get a sore face.'

149

'Give me your fucking money.'

Mitchell barely noticed him starting to pull the hand out of the pocket: he was too busy connecting squarely with the unshaven jaw. The young man crumpled into the pavement and his hand dropped the gun.

The single shot echoed down the quiet street.

The seconds in which he could have fled were eaten up by astonishment. The guy really did have a gun! The customers and barmen had looked out cautiously and then appeared in a flood. He was surrounded by a congratulatory mob when the instinct to run finally seized him.

POLITIE. Too late. The two officers who strolled from the patrol car were like twins. Same medium height, same neat moustaches, same clear English. One arranged the ambulance for the dishevelled mugger with the self-inflicted wound in his leg and took over the crowd. The other one handled Mitchell.

'It's all right. We know him – from the Zeedijk. He's in violation of a deportation order amongst other matters. You are a brave man but perhaps lacking in caution.'

Mitchell didn't have to feign his amazement.

'I can't believe it. I didn't know he really had a gun.'

'The Zeedijk is a much-quietened place but it still has its cowboys.'

Mitchell explained about his flight, tried to flash the highlights of his new identity to the front of his brain. An old woman managed to bypass the first policeman, said something in Dutch. Mitchell's minder smiled.

'You are the local hero, Mr Fletcher. At the station house you will have good coffee and I guarantee we will clear the paperwork as quickly as possible.'

It was a test, a final hurdle. Mitchell tried to cling to his faith in Kolb. No sweat: if the documents were good enough for airport checks, they were surely good enough for the Warmoesstraat copshop.

The car purred quietly along the narrow street. On either side, the pavements crowded up as they neared their destination. But Mitchell *did* sweat, barely heard officer Mesdag's touristic commentary to the city's vice centre.

'You are agitated. I'm not surprised. But you were cool in the crisis – that's what counts.'

Afterwards, Mitchell found that he could scarcely recall the interval when he got out of the car and followed – *followed*! – the two policemen into the station. There was no clock in the cell but he guessed it must be getting on for midnight. Over and over again, his mind insisted on replaying instead the face of the third policeman. The one behind the reception desk: the one who stared at him, looked back at the picture taken with Jean on the beach at Tenerife, stared back at him a second, elated time.

Saturday

Chapter Six

'Christ, I told you last week we might be having a couple of drinks on Friday night. Isobel in accounts. Her leaving do.' It was no use: Kerr still couldn't recall the conversation. He pulled back the blanket, got up from the sofa. He knew he didn't always take in every detail but he was still certain that she hadn't said any such thing. He yawned, stretched, yawned again. He stepped carefully over the shards of glass and examined the broken frame of their wedding photo.

There was always more than one way out of a situation while it was still in the present tense. It was only after the event that one set of actions became crystallized as fact and the others turned into if onlys. He'd intended to talk rationally about leaving, maybe suggest a trial separation. She hadn't been there! Later, he'd held her instinctively: the plain relief that she'd got home safe, wasn't under a bus somewhere. It was her rejection – her retreat – that had thrown him. No, not now. No, I can't. I'm sorry.

If she'd heard the smash she'd ignored it. Either that or she'd gone straight to sleep as soon as she'd gone upstairs. The picture itself didn't seem to be damaged. Stare at a print long enough and you lose the image, get captured by the sheen and grain, the patterns of the gloss. He looked away, his eyes blinking. There was a dustpan and brush in the hall cupboard. He wanted to clear up the glass before he let the cat in. As soon as he'd fed her, he'd wash, change, get the hell out of the house and back to the Divi.

In recognition that it was Saturday, Jacobson had cleaned out the cafetière and made himself proper coffee to follow his breakfast rather than his usual, rushed instant. The kettle clicked off and he poured in the water, enjoyed the appearance of the thick, brown froth. Janice had always argued that coffee should be made with hot not boiling water. There were some undeniable minor advantages to aloneness.

His mind turned again to the unposted letter. Whoever and wherever Alison was, her reappearance had obviously been a big deal for Roger Harvey. He felt in his guts that it must be connected in some way to his murder. He also knew very well that gut instinct was a highly dangerous commodity for a detective. As an absolute minimum you had to be able to distinguish it from prejudice, subject it to due process, be prepared to drop it like a hot potato if it conflicted with the objective evidence. But none of that meant that he wasn't prepared to listen to it. The problem in this case was just that a first name and an out-of-date photograph weren't very much for him to go on.

What was he supposed to do? Step one: requisition several boxes of policemen and tuck them up with the student records of Harvey and his peers or – to be more scientific – of the three or four years on either side? Better make it every college in the city too, not just the university. He'd only been at Birmingham after all! Step two: send them out to track down the current whereabouts of each and every Alison? Even then she was just as likely to have been a waitress or a civil servant or a girl he'd met on the bus.

He shook his head at the hopelessness of it, poured himself a cup of coffee only to find there was no milk in the fridge again. He was searching the cupboards for the powdered stuff when the telephone rang. It was Kerr calling from the incident room. He'd evidently clocked on bright and early although he didn't sound much like either.

'British Telecom have got back to us re that Lake District number, Frank. Something called the Scarsbeck Community.'

The Lake Windermere filling station had been one thing, the biro-ringed place name had been another. Now, suddenly, there was a third element which might – or might not – turn the whole into a great deal more than the sum of the parts. Might or might not, something or nothing. There was only one way to find out.

When Kerr went off the phone, Jacobson gave up his search for the milk tin, decided just to settle for black coffee. He'd barely taken a sip when it rang again. Sally! In a rush, the way she always was. There was really only time for him to check when her train would get in the following evening – to tell her he'd definitely be there – and then her voice was gone, vanished. He drank the rest of the coffee, realized that he was running late himself. He hoped he'd sounded convincing anyway, hoped that he really meant it.

The word that David Mitchell was in custody in Amsterdam reached him in his office almost as soon as he got there and just as he was about to head downstairs for the morning briefing. The Dutch police had apparently contacted Scotland Yard sometime around midnight. Typically, the Met were only letting mere provincials like himself in on the secret several hours later. So bloody what if it was his suspect? The Met had claimed its traditional *droit du seigneur*, had probably proposed and then rejected Mitchell's profile for a couple of dozen unsolved cases before dropping their interest in him.

He gazed through his window into the

pedestrian precinct. Already the crowds were starting to mass towards the shopping centre, scattering pigeons and litter in their wake. Apparently Mitchell was denying that he *was* Mitchell but the Dutch weren't buying it; especially as they'd found photographs of his wife in one of his suitcases. It was good news from abroad all right but it also gave him a manpower problem. He felt strongly about the Lake District connection, intended to check it out himself. Which meant that Kerr would be needed to hold the fort here while he was gone. DC Williams and – especially – Emma Smith were impressing him as competent investigators but he'd never worked with either of them before, didn't really know their capabilities. They'd been drafted in on instant secondment from Crowby Central simply because of the usual chaos of understaffing, suspensions and sick leave. An extra strong gust of wind blew a crisp packet up all the way onto his window sill. It would have to be Barber and Mick Hume for Holland then. They were both solid and reliable enough and, if Barber was a high-flyer only in his dreams, he *did* have a bit of graduate-entry polish about him. The Dutch would probably go for that, he thought.

With his mind made up, he spent as little time as he reasonably could on the briefing and left Kerr to sort out the details of the day's division of labour. By ten o'clock Jacobson was out of Crowby and on the motorway. He'd always enjoyed long journeys alone. Shifting from station to station, playing a tape or just listening to his thoughts above the traffic noise. He'd been nearly thirty before he'd driven his own car and the combination of speed and privacy still occasionally seemed like a brave new world opening up to him.

Suddenly, or so it appeared at his steady eighty-five, he noticed a southbound jam crawling along the third lane past a bolus of police Range Rovers in military formation around half a dozen decrepit old vans and converted ambulances. Thank Christ he was headed north. A mile further on, exactly at the county border, he saw another Range Rover pulled up on the hard shoulder. Behind this one, a Day-Gloed single-decker proclaimed REALITY TOURS as its destination.

He sped uncomfortably past. Another weekend of police time tied up with an illegal gathering. Not in my bloody backyard! It wasn't the raves themselves or the weekend kids that really worked up the local media and the hack councillors but the involvement of the travellers: the prospect that they might choose the county as winter quarters, seduce some solid citizens' sons and daughters.

Jacobson really didn't want to know. Roger Harvey had been done to death and it was his duty to catch the killer just as it had been his duty to stop the Crawler. He rarely cared to acknowledge

160

how much he'd come to rely on the lofty sense of purpose which grabbed him in pursuit of a truly serious case. Today of all days he didn't want his nose rubbing in the moral ambiguity of everyday policing. The cop with his billy-club, the bleeding rioter. His mind played him a dozen unwelcome versions from around the world. Police, police, po-lice oppression: the chorus of some record from Sally's days as a punk fan.

But if I wasn't doing the job, or somebody like me, it would be somebody far worse. He scanned the radio again, seeking distraction. It was his stock defence: he'd said it and thought it so many times, he really didn't know any more whether he actually believed it or not.

Judy Keegan started to boot up the DawnTrader system and tried not to think about Robert, her boyfriend, still sleepily under the duvet, his dark curls, his body tanned and not too muscular. If there was something better in life than weekends in bed then it would almost certainly turn out to be hopelessly illegal or hopelessly expensive or both. Never mind – she liked the quietness in Pelican House without its Monday to Friday hubbub and with a bit of luck she should be able to get through this particular batch of trials in a couple of hours. It would be worth it in the long run, she hoped. David Mitchell's disappearance meant more work but it was also the chance to show what she could really do. They'd made her temporary team leader in his absence: now it was up to her to make the change permanent.

She noticed that the server seemed to be taking its time reassembling the files and directories. Anyway she could pick up another bottle of the special offer champagne and something savoury and microwaveable from Marks and Spencer on the way back. They could unplug the phone. And then they – bloody hell! It definitely shouldn't be taking as long as this. She brought the command sequence back up, checked for syntactical error or mis-keying but could not find anything wrong. In the time-honoured fashion of a progammer faced with an unexpected glitch, she switched the machine off, then switched it back on again. The server hummed and whirred in a way she didn't think she'd heard before, knew for definite she didn't like the sound of. The DawnTrader main menu flashed quickly on to the screen and just as quickly disappeared. She checked the hard drive, then the network drives. Bastard! All the core programs – every single routine and sub-routine – had gone, every single data item had vanished!

Frantically, she unlocked the cupboard which contained the physical back-up, a shiny set of seven cds. At some level she already knew it was hopeless, already knew that only David Mitchell had both the access permissions and the degree of skill for a stunt like this. Six of them were completely blank, completely useless. The seventh contained just the kind of calling card she would have expected from a wanker like that: a doctored version of *Tomb Raider* with Lara Croft naked and full-frontal.

Kerr pulled into the car park outside the crime scene building, saw that the Kents were waiting for him in their Volvo saloon. Like Jacobson, he wasn't expecting much to come of the arrangement but knew that it still had to be gone through. At least, he thought, it meant he could put off reaching a decision about Professor Merchant. In the wake of Jacobson's conversation with Matt Ramshaw, *somebody* needed to confront him and needed to do it soon. There was no argument about that. But Barber and Hume were sorting themselves out for Holland and Williams and Emma Smith had their hands full back at the incident room finishing off the cross-referencing of the results from the door to door inquiries. Face it, he told himself: the bullet which said go and tell one of the country's top pathologists he'd withheld evidence had the name Ian Kerr written all over it.

He unlocked the door to Roger Harvey's flat and watched Annie precede John Kent inside. The forensic procedures were now complete and an hour ago the police watch had finally been stood down. On police advice, the Kents had shelled out for the door to be strengthened and new, tougher locks fitted. Securing the gaff was one thing, Kerr thought, unearthing an unsuspecting or unsuperstitious buyer would probably be another. Harvey's will was five years old and dated to the month when he'd bought this place. It named John Kent as his executor and Annie as the alternative in the event of another untimely exit. Harvey had inherited a sizeable amount on his parents' death so that his own estate was larger than might have been expected. The will's instructions however were precise and unambiguous. His academic books were to be offered to the university library; everything else was to be sold off and his total wealth was to be donated to Amnesty International: not only did none of his acquaintances stand to gain from his death, none of them were even to be left any substantial souvenir of his passing.

Kerr closed the door and moved through the narrow hall towards the lounge. The idea was that although there'd been no obvious burglary, the murderer might still have removed something from the flat. As close friends, the Kents were likely customers to clock the absence of some familiar object. They were standing hand in hand in the middle of the lounge when he reached the doorway.

Babes in the wood!

In the darkest, most dangerous part of his mind, he saw himself shoving the little husband to one side. He didn't fight the image, let its significance play on him. It was a primitive impulse, pure and impure. Standing in this room where they'd call in on him on the way to the cinema or the supermarket, it was suddenly hard to believe that the idea hadn't regularly plundered Roger Harvey's brain too.

Annie Kent took her hand away first. Kerr saw – or imagined he saw – something new and vacant in her expression. She'd revealed on the stairs that she'd finally relented to her GP's suggestion. 'Valium. I detest tranquillizers, but maybe for a few days . . .' Maybe. They didn't work for her as a nicotine substitute anyway. He watched her light one now, noticed the long, perfect, unpolished nails. Reflexively, he looked round for an ashtray, found one next to a pile of albums on the floor by the door. They'd been stacked away from the main collection for some trivial reason which would never now be fathomed. Headed for a jumble sale or a charity shop or borrowed from somebody, due for return. Maybe again. John Lee Hooker's *Mr Lucky* was the top one. It was the last album Kerr had bought on vinyl himself before he'd finally conceded that cds lasted longer and sounded better. He passed her the clean, glass ashtray, kept the irony of the title to himself.

The autopsy had suggested the lungs of a non-smoker but the post-autopsy analysis had found small traces of THC in the bloodstream. It wasn't an uncommon phenomenon; the occasional toker who never smokes a straight. Why not? It was probably an occupational hazard for a bloke like

Harvey. Annie Kent moved behind the sofa and glanced around the room. The chalked-off, blood-stained area where Harvey's body had lain was only a couple of feet away.

'No, Sergeant, there doesn't seem to be anything missing. It's . . . it's just the same as it's always been.'

Kerr kept his eyes on John Kent as he poked around, checking the dead man's few ornaments and pictures. Annie Kent was putting the ashtray down on the sofa when he called to her from the other side of the room.

'The dragon, Annie! Where's the dragon?'

The question seemed to breathe the life back into her. She scoured the lounge, the bedroom, finally the kitchen. Kerr and John Kent followed her through.

'You're right, John. It's not here!'

She drew on her cigarette, exhaled slowly, while her husband's hands revolved a wooden egg-timer as though fascinated by the tumbling, pink sand.

'It was for his birthday present back in March. He only just tolerated anyone smoking here although he, eh . . . did himself sometimes—'

Kerr already had this part of the picture, didn't press her.

'Anyway, he sometimes used to light a joss-stick to cover the smell of tobacco. So we got him a Chinese dragon, brass with a jade inlay. You use the nostrils as incense holders.'

Kerr knew the sort of thing, its size, shape, the ease with which you could grab it round the belly.

'And it was here the last time you called in?'

Kent put down the timer, gave his wife the chance for another draw.

'I'm virtually certain,' he said. 'He had it on a shelf near the fireplace if I remember correctly.'

'It sounds like an expensive gift.'

'Relatively, perhaps, but Roger was practically our oldest friend.'

Annie sat down at a pine table which could have been the little brother to the one in her own kitchen back in Wynarth. Kerr watched her bring two small pill bottles out of her bag. She checked the printed label on each and then put one of them back inside. Her hands shook as she tried to open the other one. John Kent did the job for her in the end, got her a tumbler of water too. She was distant again, medicated, when she spoke.

'I'm not very good at descriptions, Mr Kerr, but I can tell you where we bought it.'

Kerr took a note of the details and John Kent made a final tour of the flat, insisted that nothing else seemed to be missing. Kerr decided it was time to go. After he'd locked the door he handed the set of keys to Kent – officially the police were no longer responsible for the property – and they all three took the lift to the ground floor. Kerr's mobile rang as they came outside: DC Williams.

'Something's up at the company where Mitchell was working, Sarge. We've just had Tony Davies on the phone. I think Inspector Jacobson spoke to him yesterday? Anyway, the guy's tearing his hair out. Something about Mitchell ripping off software big scale.'

Kerr told him to say he was on his way. He followed the Kents' Volvo out of the estate but overtook them and left them behind as soon as they got to the ring road. In the opposite carriageway, the Christmas shopping traffic was snarling and crawling its way into town. When he arrived at Pelican House, Tony Davies virtually hauled him from his car. Kerr had heard of executive stress but now he believed in it totally, utterly. Somehow he prevailed on Davies to calm down, to keep the story on hold until they were inside and out of the wind.

Kerr had difficulty in understanding at first. He fancied that he knew a little bit about computers – he'd even used the internet once – but he wasn't getting how Mitchell could be responsible for something that seemed to have happened *after* he'd left the country.

'Judy Keegan and her team are looking into the nitty gritty details right now, Sergeant. It will probably take them a while. But essentially it looks like the work of a logic bomb.'

'A what?'

Davies took another mouthful of the brandy Kerr had strongly recommended for him. He'd managed to get him back into his office too, even managed to get him to sit down.

'A logic bomb, Sergeant,' Davies repeated. 'It's code buried inside the software you want to attack. If it's well enough hidden it could sit there harmlessly for days, weeks, even months. Completely undetectable unless you suspect it's there *and* you know how to look for it.'

'And in the meantime everything goes on working as normal?'

'Exactly, Sergeant – until the trigger event takes place inside the system. Usually the trigger is just a specific date or time. We're pretty confident that's what happened in this case. The clock gets to nine o'clock this morning or whatever and boom: the whole fucking system starts to dismantle itself. Judy reckons she was actually there when it happened—'

Davies took another deep swig; it seemed to be doing him some good – at least temporarily.

'Although of course she was too late to stop it.'

Kerr stood up and walked over to Davies' wall-sized window. You could see the whole of Crowby from up here, assuming you'd want to.

'So what you're saying, Mr Davies, is that someone has destroyed the, ehm, DawnTrader system from the inside and you reckon it was David Mitchell.'

'Who else? Judy Keegan and maybe Sanjit Patel just about have enough technical skill: but neither of them have legged it abroad, have they?'

'But why?'

Davies finished off the brandy, looked like he was about to burst into tears.

'Why? I'll tell you why, shall I, Sergeant? David fucking Mitchell isn't some spotty hacker taking a pop. If only! No. David fucking Mitchell is a smooth operator who's more than likely *copied* the entire system before he disappeared; who's more than likely sold off my company's product – my company's future – to the highest bloody bidder.'

Kerr tried to look more sympathetic than he felt. It was sod all to him if the Eschaton fat cats were out of pocket. In point of fact their loss was the inquiry's gain: an additional set of reasons for compelling Mitchell's extradition back to Crowby. He took his leave of Davies as swiftly as the public relations factor allowed, decided he'd earned himself a breather – especially in view of his next official destination.

It was more or less an impulse to call in. He was driving past anyway, he could surely spare ten minutes. The quiet cul-de-sac was the antithesis of the Bronx and the Son of the Bronx. Neat gardens, no litter and fully taxed cars. Tom Kerr was probably its last council tenant. Everybody else had long since exercised their right to buy.

He turned the sprightly-oiled gate, noticed the orderly row of rose bushes cut back for winter.

His father was already in the front doorway.

'Come in, stranger.'

He followed him into the kitchen, sat down at the table which was forever covered with newspapers, agendas, bulletins of this, committee minutes of that. The remains of a solitary breakfast – a plate and a cereal bowl – rested on a pile of newly printed leaflets. Kerr caught the slogan underneath. PENSIONERS DEMAND LOWER HEATING COSTS.

'Still the old campaigner?'

'You should know me by now, son.'

But Kerr had known him then. The endless Saturday afternoons when he'd read every comic twice through and the rain fell down in sheets. He'll be home soon, son. Your dad is a busy man. What had changed was that he could read the disappointment both ways now. His own had only been earlier. A son of mine a copper, a boss's thug. Even little Rosie had grown up to be a teacher. One day we'll all do socially useful work, son. He'd even hesitated over the shift to CID when it finally came because it also meant a move back to Crowby, to a family unwelcome. The saddest thing of all was that it had taken his mother's death for them finally to meet each other halfway, to bury their differences.

'So you're on the big murder case?'

Kerr gulped on the mug of re-heated tea.

'Yes. Christ! You could run a tank into Czechoslovakia on this!'

It was an old, stale joke but he knew the old man still liked to hear it.

'I might have been many things in my day but I was never a tankie, Ian—'

He watched his father sit down slowly, wondered about his health, his failing strength.

'I read one of his books not so long ago.'

'Roger Harvey's, you mean?'

'Aye. Not bad either. He'd dug up a lot of new material about the factional fighting in Barcelona for one thing.'

'You knew him then?'

'Of course not. Ah've just got more time for reading since I retired. There'll be no need to be getting your fingerprint kit out.'

Kerr made it one all: time to blow the whistle.

'We ran into another old warhorse at Harvey's place. Name of Joe Butler.'

'Butler? Used to work for the gas board?'

'Sounds like the same guy.'

'I knew him, although not that well. He was quite a popular speaker in the thirties if it's the same one. He still had a local following when your mother and I moved down from Glasgow after the war. I think he was a card-carrier too.'

Kerr smiled at the description. The distinction between card-carriers and fellow-travellers was more old water under the bridge. It only mattered now to a dwindling number of ageing, worn-out warriors. Yet only twelve years earlier, Tom Kerr's classification in the second category had been enough to hang his son's application to the force in the balance.

Their conversation stalled, picked up, wandered. What it amounted to was that they were pleased to see each other although neither one of them would ever put it into words. Kerr thought again about Joe Butler shuffling through his photographs, submerged in his memories. He reflected that both men had been bereaved by a cause as much as by their women. He wondered how much sorrow Tom too kept hidden except from strangers.

He had to go. He was busy. He couldn't really say why it cheered him so much when his father asked him on the doorstep for Butler's address.

Elspeth Merchant was a blonde-haired, well-preserved fifty. She couldn't remember the name of the detective – Alasdair introduced her to so many when they attended police functions – but she knew he was one, knew that's where she'd seen him before. She watched him get out of the unwashed car and walk towards the front door.

Perhaps because he'd driven out via his dad's place, Kerr was hyperconscious of the elegant driveway, the professionally tended lawn, the sheer size of the property. You probably felt the world was invented for you, for the accommodation of your needs and desires, if you lived in a set-up like this. He wondered if that was how it seemed to Merchant. Despite his professional success, he was still ultimately a salaried public employee: it had been Mrs Merchant's old money which had set him up in the leafy lanes on the right side of Wynarth. Kerr listened to the quiet crunch of his shoes on the smooth gravel, suddenly noticing and rubbing the stubble on his only vaguely shaven chin. She was in the hallway before he had time to ring the bell and then she was ushering him through an inner doorway into what she probably thought of as her reception room.

'Would you care for tea while you're waiting, Sergeant?'

Elspeth's smile was direct, unaffected. It seemed Merchant wasn't at home, although he was expected back any minute.

'I'm afraid my husband drove over to the playing fields to watch Peter. It's his first game this season for the first fifteen. Alasdair has big hopes for him as a sportsman.'

After she went out to make good the offer of tea, he sat down on the edge of an art deco chaise-longue. It complemented someone's stylish concept of the interior superbly but it turned out to be as comfortable as a park bench.

He stood up again quickly and looked through the leaded squares of window just in time to catch the glint of the returning Porsche at the distant gateway. Here comes the status wagon! The thought was his but the tone could have been his father's. Kerr's work had given him an infallible mental notebook of car makes and models but, on a personal level, his only demand was that they started when you stuck the key in.

He wondered about Cathy again, what she was doing. She hadn't answered his phone call on the way over here. What would she make of Elspeth with her three sons, her looks still intact on the verge of middle-age, her famous husband? He watched her bring in a tea set which matched the impossibly delicate blue of her dress and then go out into the hall, closing the door behind her. He could hear the murmur of two voices but couldn't make out what was being said. He poured himself out a cup of tea and immediately regretted it. The teapot might have been authentic Spode but the tea was even more stewed than his father's. He managed to empty the contents of the cup into the pot of a rubber plant just before Merchant himself stuck his head around the door.

'Let's talk in my study, Sergeant, and leave Elspeth in peace.'

Police underlings rarely registered for long on Merchant's perception as they came and went through the workaday areas of his consciousness. Kerr was an exception solely on account of the fuckability of his wife. It had been the police ball, last year or the year before. Chivers had made the introductions in passing and then he'd plied his charm into a brick wall for two or three minutes when hubby had gone off to the bar. It was probably because the smile had been meant to exclude him, to suggest to him what he'd no chance of getting, that he could recall it so clearly: the pink-and-white-and-redness of the moist tongue darting across teeth and lips. It hadn't really troubled him – he rarely pursued reluctant players – but now the keeper of all that hands-off loveliness was drinking Elspeth's tea, enduring her politeness like a fund-raising vicar. Afterwards, he realised that it was probably this hidden link to his secret life which held back his instinctive sarcasm, his annoyance at a Saturday intrusion.

He led his visitor along the hall and into a cosier, homelier room. They sat down facing each other in red leather armchairs: an old boy and a new boy in the club lounge. He placed Kerr in his thirties, labelled him bright, not a plodder. He offered him port, brandy or whisky and wasn't surprised to be turned down. This detective seemed more than smart enough to realize when a clear head was called for.

Merchant guessed what was coming. He wondered whether Jacobson had deliberately delegated the task to the younger man. Spare me the judgement of my peers. Even then, it was the coincidence of Kerr's wife which tilted the balance. He needed a confessor who knew about screwing, about how you might get to the stage where it sometimes seemed like the sole reason for staying alive.

*

Emma Smith declined the offer of a mug of tea and bought herself a chocolate biscuit and an apple – virtue following vice. She would never voluntarily have put herself in the company of Barry Sheldon but her consolation was that ten minutes interviewing also equalled ten minutes less cross-checking. Sheldon was conversely making the most of this unanticipated proximity and had nabbed a table near the cash desk in the busiest part of the canteen.

She watched him pull his chair in close, lean his elbows almost halfway across the table.

'There was nothing to see when we got there. The street was quiet as a grave.'

His dome-head and his close-cropped hair made him the personification of a copper in an anarchist's cartoon. There was nothing he could do about that but his blue, ogling eyes and his permanently leering smile were entirely his own responsibility: she pulled her own chair back by an equivalent distance.

'And you're sure it was Laura Gregory you spoke to at the refuge?'

According to the Crowby Central records, Sheldon's patrol car had been the one which had answered the report of a prowler at the Crowby Women's Refuge in the early hours of Monday morning.

'No question about it. We're called round there two or three times a month on average for this sort of caper. Sometimes we catch 'em, mostly we don't.'

Not surprising, Emma thought, if you studied the response rate to this type of incident. Sheldon and his mucker had got there inside five minutes; practically a record and probably pure coincidence. At least he was behaving himself verbally. So far there'd been no reference to the Escaped Fanny Farm or to lesbians in boiler suits.

'And you didn't notice anything unusual in the refuge or about Ms Gregory herself?'

'I can't say as I did. According to my incident sheet, she told us she'd been up late talking to one of her ladies and thought she'd noticed a figure hanging around across the street. When he was still there after five minutes, she put through an emergency call.'

She finished her biscuit and scrunched the wrapper up into the ashtray. She decided to save the apple for later.

'You checked the area, then?'

Sheldon's smile disappeared momentarily.

'I have been doing this job for some time. There was nothing three streets either side. Most probably he was in a car and was just lucky enough to take off at the right minute.'

She could only concede the point. Sheldon was a sexist bastard but there was no known reason to doubt his efficiency.

'OK. Thanks for your help. If you do recollect anything later—'

'You'll be the first to hear if I do, Detective Smith. Emma isn't it? You can ca—'

'Call you Barry? I could call you lots of things, Constable Sheldon, but most of them you'd find physically impossible.'

She was on her feet and on her way before Sheldon's sluggish Friday-night-in-the-boozer brain was able to form a reply. Compared to the prospect of another minute with Sheldon, the notion of more desk-bound paperwork suddenly seemed positively inviting.

Albert Peck was sure he hadn't been seen but if he had, so what? There were a hundred and one plausible reasons why an owner might have asked him to check inside their craft or which could be offered up if such an owner queried his presence. He'd hardly pick Saturday lunchtime if he was up to anything untoward now would he? He started in the galley, working sternwards, searching carefully in drawers, storage areas.

He wore gloves, thick ones, although he was well aware of the limitations of this precaution: Locard's Principle of Exchange, every contact leaves a trace. He'd loved all that stuff ever since he was a kid, still took the crime magazines in the shop.

They didn't sell so well as they'd used to of course; nowadays most folks seemed to prefer what they could see on video instead. He'd always preferred the written word himself. The back bedroom, his brother's room, had always been piled high with *Detective Monthly* and *True*

Crime, rich with the odour of cheap ink. The whole family had liked to follow the big cases. Obviously, he'd lost a bit of interest when they'd stopped hanging the culprits: but even so he liked to keep up.

He opened the drawer in which underpants and knickers had been promiscuously mixed. That Crowby detective hadn't been after an unpaid fine. Not a bit of it! And what was a handsome woman like that doing with a stuck-up little runt in the first place? There was something funny there all right. Did they think he didn't know they tried to avoid him in the bar? It was after Kerr had gone and he'd checked the unsold pile of John Kent's books that the connection had finally clicked into place.

He resisted the temptation to linger over the sight of Mrs Kent's panties. This was a serious business: Kent worked in the same place as the murdered man who'd been in the papers!

Chapter Seven

The last part of the cracked road which led to the Scarsbeck Community wound through the canopy of a small wood. Jacobson slowed to a crawl, watching another leaf shiver in the wind as it clung transiently to the wiper blade.

Burnished red, bronze, golden yellow; the colours in his vocabulary didn't seem any kind of match for the colours his eyes followed in the scurries and flurries of the leaves or even for the bare black branches they'd left behind. No wonder poets hid behind metaphor, never tried to drink autumn neat.

At the edge of the wood, the road twisted over a running stream and followed the curve of a grey stone wall to the first of the Scarsbeck buildings. Jacobson pulled up by an outhouse which so far had escaped the attention of the old farm's new renovators. Lichen clung greenly to a rusty pipe which careered up what remained of its most intact side.

He got out of the car and pulled on his over-coat. Glad I brought this. He was about to set off towards the main buildings when he stopped and turned as if some suddenly important thought had entered his mind. He pocketed his hands against the cold and looked back across the roof of the woodland. From this distance, it was a dark mass against the pale sky. He sniffed the air, felt the silence of a landscape on the cusp of winter. For a moment, there was no murder investigation, no Crowby, no Frank Jacobson middle-ageing and alone.

He knew trees about as well as he knew colours so he couldn't say what kind of tree the hawk landed in. It was only a guess too that it was a buzzard. He sniffed the air a second time. He ought to be getting bloody on with it now he was here! The hawk was sitting stock still. Another minute would not hurt.

There had been a wilder early time when the community had pursued a wilder, ecstatic vision. The focus then had been Gurdjieff, neo-Sufism and even Crowley. There had been a shunning of publicity, a belief that those attuned to their work would be drawn to them in any case, would always turn up when the time was right. Times had changed: the wild men and wild women neglected bills, bungled at practicalities, antago-nised the local council. Amongst themselves they fought and quarrelled. Finally they left.

Now the community advertised its courses,

offered you cassette tapes, designed professional-looking brochures and calendars of events. If you wanted to, you could also read its audited and healthy yearly statement of accounts. The latest publicity video was winding smoothly to an end on a flat-screen television when Jacobson entered Community Reception, an area that had once been the front parlour of the original farmhouse.

The room had the air and the layout of its equivalent in any pleasant, mid-range hotel. Down the hall, the original kitchen had been widened and brightened into a cafeteria area. As the ambient soundtrack faded close by, Jacobson could hear Van Morrison coming from the larger room. He recognised the voice from the previous evening, the cd he'd borrowed from Kerr. The song was something about Avalon, the voice was older, deeper, even more arresting. Innocence and experience: he'd never read Blake but somehow the distinction fitted the bill. The music seemed to leave a gap in the air when it finished.

Lila, a tall Australian, was one of the three Visitors' Facilitators. She listened smilingly to Jacobson's request but her answer was evasive.

'I really think you need to meet with Peter. Our guests trust us with a great deal of themselves. Confidentiality is a big issue here.'

He watched her go off in search of the Community Director. Even when you disguised it with labels of your own invention, you couldn't seem to get away from the human reliance on hierarchy. It was a depressing thought after the hawk and the wood and the song.

He'd always blessed the fact that the force's power structure was open, up front. He knew he could never stand the scuttling camouflage of politeness which authority wore in civilian organisations; smile while I screw you. Inside one part of Chief Inspector Jacobson was a man that the raging, failing, original Scarsbeckians would have hailed as brother.

He walked over to the window, looked across to the building which the map on the back of the brochures called the Old Barn. Jacobson had studied a copy closely but there hadn't seemed to be a corresponding new barn anywhere. The barn doors had been painted a deep green. You could hear the genuinely old-fashioned creak as they opened slowly and a small group of figures emerged into the neatly swept courtyard.

He hoped the situation wouldn't turn difficult. The community had no legal option except to hand over whatever records they kept of both visitors and full-time members but if they didn't want to cooperate, they could cost him any amount of delay. Worse, he'd need to call in the local side who were quite likely to take offence at his highly previous appearance on their patch. Typically, he'd persuaded himself that he hadn't had time to make the statutory notification. Circumventing the proper channels: it was quicker until it was slower.

There were half a dozen of them, three men and three women. The oldest-looking man walked quickly in front, setting the pace. Grey-hair, grey-beard, gold-rimmed glasses, his paunch propelling the front of a yellow kaftan-style shirt. Maybe he was another leader-in-disguise or maybe he was just in a hurry. He watched as the others came closer too. Lila came back, announced that Peter would be along any minute. But by then Jacobson no longer needed to worry about his meeting with the Community Director or whether he could persuade him to cough up names and dates in the absence of a warrant.

The woman in the centre of the group was dark-haired and smiling. It was November in Cumbria so she wasn't in her bikini but she was Mrs Jean Mitchell just the same.

She'd felt so calm crossing the courtyard, everything falling into place, knowing it had been the right decision to come here after all. This was when and where she would awake from the years of deadening, life-denying slumber.

It had started long before the accident, she saw that now. It was as if she'd driven herself underground, leaving only her robot-self in charge to deal with the shopping run, the roads campaign, the garden centre. She'd played him now, the robot, in some of the gestalt sessions. For he was a him, sitting on her energies, passions. Stony-faced, automatic: controlled, minimum response.

The group had been with her the other day when she'd buried him, limb by metallic limb, amongst the trees they'd dubbed the Wildwood. Small creatures would find a winter home in his empty pistons, his battery heart. They'd danced round the oak afterwards, heard the thundercrack of a bolting squirrel in the high branches.

She'd known it was bad news as soon as she'd seen him in the hall. Bulky, authoritative, official. It didn't matter. Her heart was open. She could deal with it.

The cafeteria was actually the Green Buddha Café. Jacobson sat at a window seat, close to the indoor fountain. He heard the water gurgle and trickle as he nursed a glass of apple juice. There'd been fresh, strong-looking coffee behind the counter but somehow it was the juice he'd wanted. Out in the garden, a gaggle of drummers and dancers ignored the gathering clouds.

He checked his watch. He'd give her another five, ten minutes. She'd been shocked. Yes, but imperturbably shocked – if that made sense. He couldn't recall anything like it. There'd been no anxiety in her request for a few minutes on her own. Jacobson could move swiftly into the rhythms of a situation. She didn't need it so she could have it. He'd watched his wider audience visibly relax when he'd given his approval. When to tread carefully, when to fly in: he'd yet to see that kind of decision, the experience it fed on, codified by the crime management theorists.

Big deal. He'd smoothed the preliminaries but he was still going into the main event with a minimum of preparation. The wife of the chief suspect was an unknown quantity, a paid-up member of a highly prized club: private citizens Not Known To The Police. They'd checked up on the hit and run of course. No one had said a word but he'd read it in every face on the team. Suppose the driver hadn't been caught ... suppose that Harvey ... suppose that Mitchell!

No dice. Nelson had scotched the notion in his first report. They'd caught the driver inside twenty-four hours and chucked more than one book at him. Cast-iron forensic evidence and non-mitigating circumstances: a recidivist celebrating a giro snatch from his local post office with nine pints of lager and a stolen hot hatch. The Mitchells might have seen eighteen months for the accident as derisory but then you had to think about the three years for the robbery and the non-concurrent seven for the car-jack-in-the-plastic-bag 'gun'.

Jacobson finished his drink just as the downpour burst. The dancers started to run, the drummers struggled with their instruments. Some might see retribution as consolation but his instant snap was that Mrs Mitchell wasn't one of them.

She tried to compose herself, ready herself for

this unexpected contact with the outside world. Whatever it was she knew it was bad, serious. Why else would they send a policeman all the way here from Crowby? But she knew too that whatever it was she would draw strength from being here, from the community.

She let her mind drift for a moment, put herself back in the Old Barn with the rest of the group. Not all of the lines they'd used today had been the ones she'd given them. Some of them had improvised, found more salt for the wounds.

'You should be ashamed of yourself after all we've done for you.'

'Oh love is it? That won't pay the rent.'

'Dirty little bitch.'

She'd circled within their circle, swum against the rising tide of voices.

'We should never have let her go.'

'All that education. A bloody waste.'

Their faces had blurred: Carl, Marsha, Sarah, Carl again. They'd locked arms, making their circle smaller, their voices louder.

'Bitch.'

'Waste.'

'Education.'

'She'd better have an abortion,' one of them had shouted and the others had taken the word up, turned it into a chant.

'A-bortion. A-bortion. A-bortion.'

She'd pushed against them then, screamed, let all her anger go – all of it.

She decided to put on something warm. Maybe they could walk in the grounds while they talked. She was understood here, listened to, appreciated. She was strong now, unafraid. Whatever David had done, whatever the policeman wanted to know, she promised herself she would stay that way.

The cloudburst had ended but the gardens were still wet with rain. They passed out of the café on to the terrace and across the broad sloping lawn. Jacobson found himself amongst rockeries, lily ponds and once-formal borders all at various stages of dreamy transformation towards the Scarsbeck ideal of cultivated wildness. He was still treading gently – establishing uncontroversial facts, emphasizing that nothing was certain at this stage. They simply needed to speak to Mr Mitchell; nobody was in a position to say he'd definitely done anything.

Their path brought them to a thicket of winter jasmine. Mrs Mitchell stopped. She broke off a small stem bearing three slender yellow flowers and fixed it to the brooch on her green poncho. She was smaller than the stills had made her appear. When she stood back up, her head just about came to Jacobson's shoulders. He asked her about the low, oval building which lay up ahead, sheltered under an ageing tree he dimly believed to be a silver birch.

'That's our meditation house.'

She explained the difference between the meditation house and the big meditation hall in the building behind the Old Barn. Community space and personal space: as many guests and members as wanted to could share the morning and evening meditations in the hall; the house provided for a more personal focusing of energies. You could go there any time in twos, threes, fours or, more commonly, alone.

Mrs Mitchell checked through the recessed window for the unlit candle.

'It's OK. Nobody's using it. We can look in if you like.'

'I won't need to chant or anything will I?'

He wasn't sure if she saw the joke, didn't entirely know if he'd made one.

'No. Just the opposite. You mustn't disturb the silence.'

The meditation room had a small antechamber where Jacobson was persuaded to remove his shoes and where he therefore inferred that conversation was still permitted.

'The main thing, Mrs Mitchell, is that your husband seems to have known the victim. Not only that – he was also his neighbour.'

He took out the photograph of Harvey, handed it to her, watched it fall out of her hand. Jean Alison Mitchell's scream would have broken the silence in the Potala Palace.

Emma Smith finished her apple, the bit of Laura

Gregory's alibi still irritatingly between her teeth. The Divi had routinely logged her call at 2.03 am on automatic diversion from the busy Central numbers. Too bad she'd tried to phone direct! If she'd gone through the 999 route, there might even still have been a recording. The whole thing was watertight from the midnight counselling session all the way through to her visit from the Barry Sheldon charm school. Fuck and shit! She struck the keys randomly, ddfsgbbbbbbbbbbbb bbbbbbbbbbbbbbb, watched the last letter – the b – rapidly fill the screen.

Even the existence of the register was no help. It had one straightforward page per night duty. You filled the times in at the top and signed and dated it at the foot. In between, you could leave it blank in the absence of any significant incident or interaction. When she'd looked through, approximately half the pages had been exactly like that: clean sheets. Suppose she got a warrant and sent it off for ESDA testing? It would come back looking just as kosher whether it had genuinely been made out during the night in question or at some later time. ESDA could tell you if something had been removed from a written record, it couldn't tell you *when* an entry had been made. Shit and fuck! You'd have to be as devious as an assistant chief constable to put a suspicious gloss on the fact that most of the time only Laura Gregory herself would bother to read the register. Maureen had called her the enthuser, the inspiration. Her day-in, day-out commitment naturally made her the woman who'd check the book in the morning and brief the nightshift – when it wasn't herself! – in the evening.

All of which brought you back to Jackie Wilkinson. She cleared the screen and re-accessed the details: three cautions and three convictions, all for soliciting. In her mind, she could still see the long, straight hair, the almost angelic face. The bruises on her arms and legs had needed medical attention the last time she'd been pulled in but Joe, the pimp-cum-husband, had still gone unfingered. 'Laura sat up with me till after one, she made me coffee.' It was the one possible weak spot all right: the testimony given in gratitude. Are we, members of the jury, to accept the word of a common prostitute? Shit and fuck and shit! Hhasehaehsewtfhasrwefyuzcb! At this rate, she was going to break the keyboard. Whatever the right-on sisters might have thought about the women in the force, it was a line of inquiry which Emma Smith was seriously tempted to bury. DC Williams filed the last of the door-to-door statements, asked her what was on her mind. She knew as he did so that she had only two real choices: follow it through or resign.

A quarter of an hour later, they parked up across the street in time to see Laura Gregory emerge down the front steps and quickly drive off in a green and white 2CV. When they knocked on the door, Emma was relieved to find that Maureen wasn't on duty either. Instead, a tall, matronly woman showed them in. She seemed polite, almost welcoming, but she still reminded Jackie Wilkinson of her rights and peppered the air with the names of a good third of the Police Committee before she reluctantly left them to it.

Emma fingered the brocade on a piece of black velvet. It was almost exactly twenty-four hours since she'd called here on her own. The twins were asleep again, there was more work on the sewing table and the same afternoon light fell unruffled through the attic window.

'Do you actually manage to sell any of this stuff?'

'I do all right. My sister has a stall at the Saturday market in Wynarth.'

Williams got into the stride of it quickly.

'But not well enough, eh? Or is it just too much like hard work?'

His voice came across loud and hard-edged. Like his frame, it seemed too big for the dimensions of the room. Jackie Wilkinson put her work to one side, looked from Williams to Emma and back again.

'I don't know what you're talking about.'

Emma watched his mouth broaden into a sneer.

'The game is what I'm talking about, Jackie,

and you back on it. There's an elderly gent in ward ten of the General who was found wandering round Clarence Street last night with his pants down and his head bleeding. He never saw his assailant but he did get a very good look at the bait. He seemed very interested when we showed him your face in the slag book.'

'You fucking liar! I never left here all night. Any of the girls will tell you. Laura—'

'So Laura Gregory's your alibi? That's a convenient arrangement what with you helping her out the other night. I take it you remember your last social inquiry report? The next time you're nicked these two are taken into care for good.'

Williams stared at the pink cots. The girl stood up, her tiny white knuckles clenched somewhere between anger and fear.

'You bastards! You know I wasn't anywhere near Clarence Street don't you? I don't want to lose the boys and I don't want to go inside but I'm not going to help you fit up Laura either. She was with me on Sunday night just like I said.'

It had been Emma Smith's initiative all the way through. She was even quieter than Williams on the drive back to the Divi. Jackie Wilkinson had certainly revealed her strength of feeling for Laura Gregory. Fine: but their exercise in scaled-down nastiness hadn't brought them any closer to knowing whether she was telling the truth or not.

*

The woman called Marsha found two glasses and a dark green mug next to the sink.

'She's not in shock clinically, if that's what you mean. A sedative would dull the edges but it's healthier in the long run just to experience what you're feeling. I've a bottle of whisky and a box of ciggies in my suitcase – I'm prescribing both.'

Jacobson couldn't fault her diagnostic skills. If your husband is likely to become a murder suspect in the middle of your solstice-to-solstice retreat then room-sharing with a qualified doctor comes highly recommended. One: cut down your accommodation costs. Two: have a professional on tap when the CID call by.

Jacobson had quite unconsciously bagged the deepest armchair. He took out his own cigarettes and proffered the pack.

'Not for me, just the patient.'

She poured two medium measures into the glasses and a large one into the mug.

'Do you want some water in here, Alison?'

Mrs Mitchell was sitting on the side of her bed. The heating had been turned on full and the colour was returning to her face.

'No, no. I'll have it just as it is.'

She took the mug from Marsha and the cigarette from Jacobson.

'Can Marsha stay with us?'

He put the cigarettes back in his pocket without taking one himself. So far, he'd made no move towards the whisky glass either.

'Of course. Just take it easy and take your time.'

She wasn't sure how much was for the policeman, how much for Marsha, how much for herself. Drink and talk. Talk and drink. She'd been in a room burdened with sudden, unexpected death before. Drink and talk. Talk and drink. She'd sat with sympathizing, reassuring listeners before. Not easy to listen but easier: then and now, it wasn't happening to them. Drinking and talking and shouting and roaring – pummelling futile punches into David's hard, strong chest. Child or adult, the mourning of death followed a common course.

'One thing I know, one thing I can say: it's not me, not that I'll never see him alive again, it's what he'll never see, never do, never know. How can somebody just be finished? How can he just be over, gone like that? And you think that David? How? David never knew. We were so careful in the corridor ... He never knew! He wouldn't care anyway. He didn't care! He would have laughed. His cruel laugh, his everything-I've-done laugh. Yes, of course it was before I was married, before David. I was barely twenty for Christ's sake. They thought they'd talked me into it but it was MY decision – I didn't want the baby. I never told him, never asked him. Only afterwards it felt like a betrayal. I couldn't be with him anymore. He never guessed why at the time. Oh, they so much thought they'd won when I left the university and came back to them; the darling daughter returned from ruination amongst the communists and anarchists – and then when I met David, married him: oh, she's settled down now, the lass. But they hadn't won, I'd just given up, stopped trying. When my son was born, it was like it didn't matter anyway, there was something important to do, this connectedness to life . . . and then the thread broke again. That was when I noticed just how much I actually hated David, every bloody thing he stands for. He's the last prick on earth I'd have another child with.'

She felt the glow of the whisky all the way down to her stomach, clenched the mug tightly. He'd seemed so cautious, comically unsure, untying the laces of his scuffed black brogues in the meditation house. Now he passed her a second cigarette and then had to take it back, light it for her with his solid steady hands. As soon as you arrive, you're headed somewhere else.

'See, a funny thing is I'd started to get it together before I ran into him again. It was all dead with David, his thoughtless greed, his cynicism, his stupid, boorish views. I'd already decided to come here, a final break between an old life and a new one. Meeting Roger again, it was like just another sign that I was reconnected, tuning back in. I only saw him a couple of times. We both knew it was too late to start again. There are some things you break that can never be mended. It was more like we had the chance to straighten it between us, get ready to move on to the next phases in our lives. Christ, there was so much for him: his book, California.'

Jacobson sampled the whisky at last but slowly watched Jean/Alison sobbing quietly against Marsha's big sister hug. He let five minutes pass before he forced his mind back into police mode.

'This first time you heard from Dr Harvey again. How did that come about?'

'It was in the middle of September – just after my birthday.'

'He just turned up on your doorstep?'

'No, he phoned me. Late on a Monday night. It was like hearing a voice down a time tunnel. Mondays became our regular phone night for a while. It seemed like there was so much to say, to catch up on. He wanted to see me straightaway but it was a couple of weeks before I agreed. We had a day out in Birmingham. He met me off the train at New Street. Platform nine! He always used to be there when I came back from a weekend at home. For a minute, I had this daft fantasy that he'd been waiting there for me all these years.'

'You said you only met a couple of times?'

'Three times in fact. He drove me up here last

month and we spent two nights at a hotel near Windermere just before the start of the retreat. The third time was only last week—'

A battalion of neurons flashed 'Thursday' in Jacobson's brain but he kept the thought to himself.

'Thursday, I don't know how it happened really. One minute I was sitting in the café with the rest of the group, talking, laughing. Then it was suddenly as if I had to get away. It was like the bit inside you that resists any change or risk was fighting back, asking me what I was doing here with all these strangers. I just sort of wandered off. Somehow there was a taxi and then there was the railway station and I was phoning Roger, asking him to meet me when I got to Crowby.'

'When exactly did you phone him, Mrs Mitchell? It could be important.'

'Oh, I'm not sure. Five o'clock, maybe. I remember the train got in about twenty past ten and Roger was waiting for me.'

Jacobson drained his whisky, decided to award himself his first cigarette of the afternoon.

'So you spent Thursday evening at Dr Harvey's flat?'

'Yes, that's what I meant about being careful in the corridor. It was dark when we drove out there and we never saw a soul in the building. We virtually crept into the flat without saying a word. I don't see how David could have known we were there. He would have been at work when we left in the morning.'

'Which was when?'

'Around ten, I think. I was very tired. We'd spent nearly the whole night talking. Eventually Roger persuaded me or I persuaded myself that I ought to go back to Scarsbeck, give it a second try. So we got back in his car and he drove me up here. I don't drive myself you see, not since Oliver's accident. It was after one when we got here and he left more or less at once. I . . . I didn't know it would be the last time I'd see him alive.'

He watched the tears welling in her eyes again. He wanted to finish this soon, to leave her with her friend and the whisky bottle.

'What made him get in touch with you after such a long time? Did he ever say how he found out where you were living?'

A smile crossed her face and momentarily she was the untroubled woman on the holiday beach again.

'David landed a contract in Crowby and unknowingly rented a flat in the same building where Roger was living. I visited him there a couple of weeks after he moved in and Roger just happened to look out of his window at the right moment – or the wrong moment, I suppose – just happened to see us in the car park. Most people would describe it as chance or coincidence, I guess: here we call it syncronicity. Roger decided he wanted to make contact. He deliberately struck up a friendship with David and found some innocuous reason to get his home number. I remember David phoning me the night I got back from Birmingham and telling me about this good mate he'd made where he was living, how they'd taken to going running together. If only he'd known!'

'And you're sure he didn't?'

'As sure as I can be. Anyway, like I said, I doubt if he would have cared. I don't think he believed me at first when I said I was coming here and that I was thinking about leaving him altogether. When he did finally believe it, I think he was glad, relieved to be getting me out of his life. The bastard hasn't phoned or written once all the time I've been here.'

Albert Peck was a tall but unremarkable figure amongst the consuming swarm. In the Central Plaza, a crowd of them waited for the display clock to do its turn. Above the head of a giant imitation crow, electronic messages zapped leftwards. YOUR CHRISTMAS COUNTDOWN: 32 SHOPPING DAYS TO GO. Underneath the big, bright yellow claws, the hands on the clock face approached two o'clock. Every hour of the commercial day, after the electronic chime, the black wings flapped the air while the beak synched to the jingle about Crowby and its happy shoppers. The neat bit, the thing the kiddies loved, was that the beak also gave out hundreds of bubbles which could be chased or jumped at or just counted as they floated through brief moments of existence towards their doom on the plate glass of Next or River Island.

Peck bypassed the clockwatchers and headed into Flowers Way, convincing himself he was headed in the right direction. He rarely left the canalside these days. Even if not everybody there estimated him at his true worth, they knew his name, recognised his role. Here, or in any other big town like it, he was just another oldish, solitary man to rush in front of and ignore. Not to worry! He could be back in an hour, should certainly be on time to open up the shop.

He walked on briskly, ignoring the too-easy solution of a yellow information kiosk. The whole strategy was that he'd never been here before and would go unnoticed now. If he could, he aimed to get in and out without opening his mouth in the slightest conversation. The way he saw it he couldn't be too careful. After all, there was a real risk to his employment if the snooping came to light. He was having fun in any case: enjoying a chance to play the detective game for real, even if it was only for an afternoon. Best of all though was what it would do to the Kents themselves. They'd taken him for an old fool. Well Albert Peck could still put something over on somebody when the need arose.

Burtons, WH Smith, something called Benetton. The names flashed by him like the shoppers and then he saw that he'd been right after all: the public toilets loomed directly ahead below another electronic message board. THE CROWBY CENTRE: FOR CENTRAL SHOPPING. He went inside, catching his breath on the stench of stale urine. He didn't know why it should have surprised him: the façade was all that mattered in places like these. If you couldn't see it, it didn't count. A drunk with his hands futilely inside a broken hand dryer cursed himself or the world in general in a low monotone. He found a vacant cubicle but had to hold the door shut with his foot since the lock had been long ago carved away. This unexpected problem meant that phase one took five minutes rather than the scheduled two. By the time it was completed, the drunk had escalated to head-butting the machine and occasionally the wall behind it.

Peck made his way to the exit and to what he regarded as a proper, outside street. Another five minutes to the car park and the start of phase two. He rubbed his gloved hands together against the cold. Two lads finished Big Macs and dropped their cartons and paper bags almost at his feet. He ignored them as he'd ignored the drunk, concentrated instead on his mental rehearsal of the phone call he'd make from the edge of town. Just give the bare facts then hang up. That's right, officer, the third from the entrance, wedged behind the cistern.

The policeman had gone and she'd asked Marsha to leave her on her own. The talking and the whisky had done their work for now. She walked over to the window and looked down into the courtyard and across to the Old Barn. In an hour or so, it would start to get dark again. It actually got truly dark here away from street lights and a million lighted windows. You could watch the stars, count the constellations. It was just the opposite of what she was craving. Sanitized, artificialized, urban darkness was woven deep into the fabric of the pictures in her mind. Their rushed walks home through crowded streets, holding hands against the cold, watching the breath curl on his lips as he talked to her ceaselessly, urgently. Their first winter, their best times, their only time. Their street wasn't even physically there anymore. They'd found that out back in September. The whole area had been knocked down, demolished. As far as they could work it out, the inner expressway cut straight through the site where their building must have stood. Karim's store and the King's Arms had vanished under a waste ground which a tattered, battered poster advertised for a redevelopment which had never come. She could still see, smell and touch it all. The cramped rooms with their blue walls and the creaky bed which had embarrassed them at first. So young and so in love and so in hope: they'd even held discussion groups in the kitchen, crouched round the single-bar electric fire. Student-worker solidarity. The situation in Santiago. Later, when the others had gone, they'd settle down on the musty sofa in the company of the record player which was their only brand-new possession.

She smiled to herself, took another deep swig from the green mug. Jean before and Jean afterwards but she'd been Alison then for those two Birmingham years. It was such a bloody obvious message from the subconscious, yet she'd honestly never seen it until she'd got into personal growth, had started to pay herself some real attention. Now she was Alison again and now she'd always be Alison – even with Roger gone. She crossed the room and took her suitcase down from the top of the wardrobe. She took out the Walkman she'd never quite got round to unpacking before. She wished she'd brought a bigger player and not this child's toy with its tiny cubes for speakers. At full volume, the sound was small and fragile. Well, better than nothing. She'd called it an early Christmas present and he'd scoffed. But after he'd joked about mystical claptrap, diversions from the struggle, they'd both sat down and listened enraptured right through to the end.

She turned back to the window still seeing the dark, winter street that no longer existed. She couldn't disentangle which *Astral Weeks* she was listening to: the long-familiar songs from the Walkman or the record heard for the first time which played for ever in her memory.

Chapter Eight

At least Officer Mesdag had told the truth about the coffee. Even in the circumstances it tasted good. The food itself had been acceptable too. Lots of cheese and ham. It was the blue plastic tray and the blue plastic knife and fork that he could have done without: aircraft-style, economy class. Mitchell lay back on the short bench, wondered what the prisoner-in-transit standard would be like.

I still don't get it! Kolb had warned him about last-minute delays, difficulties. That's why he'd timed the logic bomb for Saturday morning. Eschaton *might* have checked the system when he hadn't clocked in on Thursday although somehow he doubted it. They'd struck him as a virginal set-up as far as security considerations went. Tony Davies liked to talk the talk but in reality he was full of shit, barely knew one end of a pc from the other. Mitchell had met dozens like him in his time: company men promoted way out of their depth because they licked good arse, could probably tongue crevice for the national squad. Anyway – even if they *had* – everything would still have been running smoothly then; no reason whatsoever to dig out the physical back-up. He should only have become a wanted man this morning and then only in England. 'They might not even involve the authorities, Mr Mitchell. This kind of thing is very bad for public relations, consumer confidence.' The validity of Kolb's argument had apparently vanished faster than the DawnTrader system's self-deleting files yet it still sounded persuasive. Nobody in the software industry wanted the public to know how vulnerable and precarious their products were. Eschaton, Kolb had argued, were just as likely to put a bid in for the return of the system as they were to call in the cops.

He balanced the knife and fork on top of the paper cup a couple of times. It wasn't a very challenging occupation. The Dutch had only seemed concerned for him to admit his identity, would only say that he was wanted to assist with a serious investigation in Crowby. The caffeine newly arrived in his stomach did nothing for his unease. He thought about press-ups or stretching. At this rate, he'd end up pacing the floor. Yet he needed something to do, something to keep the question out of his head: what if it wasn't just the software scam?

He looked up warily at the sudden shuffling

noise outside his cell. The door opened and the custody sergeant stepped in, his back flanked by two more officers. Like all the police he'd seen here, the three of them were armed.

'Good dinner, Mr Mitchell-Fletcher? You will come with us now and meet with your lawyer.'

The Amsterdam police had transferred Mitchell to their headquarters on Elandsgracht. Three floors further up, DCs Barber and Hume were waiting for their chance to talk to him. They'd been shown into a spacious wood-panelled room which reminded Barber of the conference suite in his previous, bored existence as a trainee company accountant. He studied the well-framed faces of the city's chiefs of police on the opposite wall. Past or present, the adjectives which sprang to mind were smiling, solid, avuncular. He didn't feel much like smiling himself. It had all looked straightforward at three thousand feet but now the reality and the difficulty of their task had sunk in. OK, Mitchell had committed an offence under Dutch law by presenting false identity papers to the police so at least he could be held securely in the short term and, yes, they'd picked up the fax of the warrant against him for the Eschaton rip-off on arrival. A case of so far so good but the thing was this: if he chose to fight extradition it could be upwards of a month before he was back on British soil. Without the completion of formal proceedings, any return was purely a voluntary matter. Barber didn't want to take bets now that the Dutch had appointed Mitchell a heavy-duty legal adviser free, gratis and for nothing.

He turned his attention from the paintings and watched the room fill up until it resembled more and more the endless meetings he'd vainly hoped to leave behind him on the force. There were two representatives from the consulate before you even counted the police themselves – half a dozen senior rankers plus two minute-taking junior officers. As they took their places round the table, Hume gave him a sly, anxious wink which matched the feeling in his own stomach precisely. Most of the rest of Barber's intake into the graduate entry scheme had long since made inspector: his career badly needed a boost like getting Mitchell on to the next plane. But just as badly it didn't need a fuck-up like having to leave him behind.

The male Dutch equivalent of a tea-lady was still dispensing coffee when Mitchell himself was brought in accompanied by his newly acquired brief. The most senior member of the home team had positioned himself directly under the imposing row of portraits. As he spoke, Barber wondered whether he was listening to Mr Next-In-Line.

'Welcome to Amsterdam, Mr Barber and Mr Hume. After questioning by my officers and in the presence of his legal representative, Mr Mitchell has at last informed us of his true identity and has agreed to speak to you in the forum of this meeting.'

Barber fingered his coffee cup but his stomach went on tightening. Maybe it would go better if he pretended to himself that he really *was* back discussing the half-yearly statement and the prospects for the next quarter.

Kerr nosed the car out of Merchant's driveway as the first drops of rain spilled on to the windscreen. A belt of rain moving south over the whole country by mid-afternoon they'd said on the radio. Sometimes the experts got it right; sometimes they got it dead wrong.

He took the case against first. One: Merchant had knowingly kept important information to himself for more than forty-eight hours. Two: he'd discussed details of the case with an outside party whom he also knew to be a possible suspect. Technically, it was obstruction as a minimum and it could add up to conspiracy to pervert. The legal niceties, old son! He could hear Jacobson's voice, knew his views on the divide between the law and common sense. They'd been on to Ms Gregory from day one anyway, had known about her affair with Harvey and the Wynarth Arms incident from day two. Merchant had been a bit naughty but the plain fact was that she would have known the circumstances at the murder scene better than anyone if she'd done it! She would have had three clear days to devise and perfect her alibi before Merchant had known a thing! You could even put an argument that his further revelations were especially helpful at this particular stage of the investigation.

Probably only a couple of weeks after the run-in at the Wynarth Arms, it seemed he'd been a witness to a virtual replay outside Humphrey's Wine Bar in Wynarth. This time Harvey had sustained a slight cut to his hand and he'd had to have it checked out at casualty. Hopefully, the hospital would still retain some record. Kerr had caught Laura Gregory on local radio more than once. He could just hear her detailing her rights under the Police and Criminal Evidence Act and declining to come to the station voluntarily. But if it came to it now, they could bring specimen charges, compel her presence on a highly-related line of investigation: belatedly, Merchant had given them the perfect excuse to haul her in, apply some real pressure.

He slowed on the sudden bend which brought you into Wynarth proper. His thoughts moved from Merchant at ease in his study to Geordie McCulloch huddled in the interview room on the first morning of the inquiry. If Geordie'd withheld the slightest evidence, there would have been no need for an internal debate. They'd have booked him for it reactively, instinctively, without a moment's fucking thought. In the case of Crowby's pathologist, even if Jacobson did decide to push it, the chances were that any charges would be expediently stymied further up the hierarchy. If they weren't, it would be a matter of which faction was in ascendancy and whether they were pro- or anti-Merchant.

Every parking space round the square was filled. He'd have to use a side street and risk a soaking. The famous career was probably safe. Jacobson's voice faded from his mind and in its place he could hear his dad, the old warrior, spitting his contempt for 'class justice'. Elspeth had been arranging flowers in the hall when her husband had shown him out. Kiss-and-tell, Kerr thought: if Laura Gregory turned out to be the suspect they sent for trial, Merchant's career might be all he'd have left to save.

The Dragon's Lair was at the end of a cobbled alley to the side of Humphrey's Wine Bar. He decided he'd try the shop first, the wine bar second. Wind chimes tinkled when he opened the door and then he had to move slowly, carefully, between the cramped aisles of fragile chinaware and the giant paper kites which hung almost in your face from the low, original ceiling. Kerr had been here earlier in the year, searching for an elusive anniversary present. It had been summer then. Now he had to wipe the rain off his face, felt the wetness seeping through his jacket and shirt and onto his skin.

She was younger, of course, but the question was whether she reminded him of Annie Kent or

213

whether Annie Kent reminded him of her.
Strangely, he wasn't surprised that she remembered him. He knew he hadn't forgotten her but
he wondered why she'd managed to stay out of
his head all this time. She asked him if he'd
found something suitable in the end, what it had
been. She told him she was only here on the odd
Saturday to give the proprietor, who was also her
landlord, the chance to see his kids. He only had
access a couple of times a month which didn't
really seem fair. Did he know Michael? It sometimes seemed as if nearly everyone in Wynarth
did. So he was from Crowby? Only she was sure
she'd seen him – them – a couple of times at the r
and b nights. He told her he – not we – drove
over to the gigs sometimes. He waited for her
attitude to change when he told her what he did,
why he was there. It didn't seem to make any
obvious difference. She had to hunt in the back-
shop to find one of the brass dragons. When she
came back, she said she recalled the purchase –
another Saturday, another coincidence. She said
she vaguely knew the Kents, she thought that
they only lived a couple of streets away from her.
Michael hadn't been able to sell very many of
them probably because of the price. She thought
they were beautiful but a little expensive. Yes,
she was sure this one was identical. Yes, she was
sure Mrs Kent had been on her own when she'd
bought it. He passed the ornament back to her,
noticing that he hadn't been wrong about its

shape and weight. She wrapped it between two sheets of white paper, each embossed with its own much smaller dragons in alternate rows of red and green. He wrote out an official receipt, assured her it wouldn't suffer any damage or if it did they'd be fully compensated. On his way out he glanced at the poster pinned near the door on a square of dark cork. Yes, it was the big night at the Blues Festival tonight: Clarence Frogman Henry. Yes, she'd always loved the blues, right since she was a teenager.

Kerr's wet hair brushed the wind chimes. Outside in the alley, the rain was still bucketing down. His mobile started to ring as he was making a dash for the wine bar.

He endured a full thirty seconds of its grating homicide of something that had once been 'Unchained Melody' while he made it through the door, wiped the rain from his face again. DC Williams repeated the message from the anonymous caller: 'It's probably another nutter, Sarge, but I thought I'd better let you know anyway.' He told him to keep it quiet for now, to meet him at the back entrance to the shopping centre in twenty minutes – no, better make it thirty.

Williams kept a watch from outside the Gents, tried not to look as awkward as he felt. Kerr held the cubicle door shut with his back and asked himself whether he really trusted his instinct. He knew he was taking a risk. If it was slight he'd find out soon, if it was big and it went wrong then it was remotely possible that he was experiencing his last moments on earth.

Strictly speaking, any call or message which referred to a hidden object in a public place should have invoked anti-terrorist procedures. The caller had asked specifically for the officers dealing with the Harvey murder inquiry, he'd used no known code word or anything that sounded like a code word; but neither fact would cut the least ice upstairs if Kerr's judgement was wrong. The building should have been cleared, the fire brigade brought in and bored policemen should have been milling around on the sidelines waiting for the army bomb disposal team to arrive. 'A letter that will interest you.' A letter! Kerr had seen a controlled explosion before. He didn't blame the army one iota for their caution but neither did he want to watch a possible lead go up in smoke just because Mr Mystery might have used an unusual brand of paperclip.

Do it or don't do it: he stood on the seat and reached up to the cistern. He took down an opened white manila envelope which had been tied with an elastic band. There was an ugly brown stain over the postmark as a result of its recent relocation but you could still make out the name and address clearly enough: Mrs A Kent, 14 Church Terrace, Wynarth. He tucked it securely in his pocket, went back outside and rejoined Williams. The crowds were seething in every direction. Kerr and Williams headed towards the stairs which led down to the exit, Kerr convincing and unconvincing himself by turns of the stupidity of the gamble he'd just got away with.

It took him ten minutes to drive his car the short couple of streets from the back of the shopping centre to the car park at the Divisional building. Williams had lost patience halfway and walked back through the rain. Kerr didn't blame him, firmly believed that one day traffic gridlock would engulf the planet, wipe out entire populations as they sat trapped behind the steering wheel.

The Divi was unusually, unnaturally quiet. Some kind of special operation was being hurriedly put together against the impending rave and there had been no shortage of volunteers more than happy to diversify from the usual Saturday overspill of town centre thieving and brawling. Kerr held a mini-briefing in the incident room. Unless Jacobson overruled it when he got back, he'd decided to bring in Laura Gregory for questioning, eliminate her – or otherwise – once and for all. He assigned Williams to get over to the hospital and check for any records of Harvey's knife injury. When he'd done that, he could pay a follow-up visit to Humphrey's. The staff he'd managed to speak to there had proclaimed glorious degrees of ignorance of any incident, anytime, but had all said that Mr

217

Humphrey – apparently there really was one – would be back in an hour, would remember something if anyone did. In the meantime, Emma Smith was to prepare the necessary paperwork. Through the soft drumming of the rain against the windows, there came the fading wheeee-oh-whio of a patrol car from a nearby street. Somebody at any rate had opted for the normal routine.

'We need to cross every t,' he told them. 'Any action we take against Right On Laura has got to be completely by the book.'

Kerr unwrapped the dragon and logged its details into the inquiry database. Enter the dragon, he thought, but decided it was too awful a pun to speak out loud. He retreated to the cramped office he shared with DS Tyler on the floor immediately above the incident room. He made himself a cup of tea which would have to be drunk black and sat down at his desk. Which was when he noticed Tyler's Post-it tip-off about the purge on unauthorised appliances. He picked up the kettle from the top of the filing cabinet and put it back in the bottom drawer, its surreptitious home. In return, he scrawled him a note concerning the empty jar of Coffeemate. Working on different cases, Tyler and Kerr could go for days at a time without meeting face to face – the yellow pad was their favoured means of communication, insult and support.

He drank the tea and moved his tannin-stained

mug well out of the way before he went anywhere near the letter. The duty soco needed to carry out a fingerprint examination before photocopies could be made. The original would then be sent on for full forensic testing. But Kerr was determined to at least glance at the contents before he let it go anywhere. It was what Jacobson would have done; it was what any detective worthy of the name would do. He already knew that the letter was addressed to Annie Kent: as he took the pages out of the envelope – holding them carefully by their edges – he understood rapidly that it had been written by Roger Harvey.

Crowby, 19th October

Annie,

I know John is still at the York conference until Thursday so hopefully it's OK to write to you – what I want to say is probably easier to write down. Also, if I write, you can read what I say more than once (conceit) and decipher the meaning.

You know I've spent a lot of time in the last year trying to make sense of my life, trying to see where I'm going. I told you that I'd met Alison again. Of all people! If she hadn't run from me back then, hadn't gone back to her cosy suburban nest, we might never have even met! – and you would never have been torn between John and me. For years it seemed to me so contemptible what she did then – so middle class! As if our time together was just play-acting, a little holiday interlude before she settled down to a proper, conventional life. Now I know I've actually been no better myself, burying myself in work, seeing nothing as it really was, pretending that what we had was only fun or consolation. I don't know if you would have, but I should have asked you to leave John after those very first times in Birmingham – or certainly in the days when you were sneaking off to see me in Newcastle. Why didn't I understand what I was feeling? Or, worse, why did I choose to ignore it? The selfish truth I suppose is that it suited me. The complication with John suited me too. I could have a share of the cake, other cakes too, and pretend there was no chance for more! You were right every time you tried to stop it. We should never have started again after the last time John put his foot down.

The other thing I need to say is that Elmwood's been in touch again, everything seems to be going according to plan out there. Yes I'm going to go. I'd like to believe it was for your and John's benefit but we all know my work always comes first with me. That doesn't mean that it isn't the best thing though, does it? We can still keep our friendship can't we, the three of us? John needs you. He always has – and especially now – but I guess you see what I'm saying about you and me. Don't think it's Alison either or anyone come to that. I just can't see the point of going on with it any more! There, I've finally said it! Can you bear our Thursday evenings for a while yet – more conceit! – John will probably think we've started up again if we stop them (irony?). Don't doubt that I loved you – it's just that I discovered it too late for it to be worth anything.

Roger

Kerr read the letter then re-read it. He was about to read it a third time when the phone rang. Jacobson's voice was barely distinct against the familiar echoing mêlée of pub talk and clinking glasses. It was almost as if you could smell the beer and choking fag ends down the line. Trust him to check into the Brewer's Rest before he checked into the incident room! Either Jacobson was packing it away too often or Kerr was just noticing it more now that he'd curbed his own boozing. The idea had been to see more of Cathy, spend less time married to the job. It struck him now as a futile gesture: too little and too late. After Jacobson rang off, he tried her at home again but there was still no reply. He undraped his still-sodden jacket from the radiator and pulled it on. It felt especially uncomfortable around the shoulders but it made him think again about the rain and

Wynarth and the girl in the Dragon's Lair.

He clicked the door shut behind him, wondering about his next step and whether – *if* – there would be a next step. Too bad Harvey was dead. He might have been just the man to call on for suitably experienced advice.

It took Jacobson and Kerr quarter of an hour each to recap on the latest events and discoveries. Then they lapsed into a localised silence as both of them absorbed a new set of angles and possibilities. Beyond their table, the Brewer's Rest was as smoky on the nose and the eyes as it had sounded to Kerr on the telephone, although it turned out to be a lot quieter. It was that part of the afternoon when the shoppers were setting off for home and Saturday's big night out was still a couple of hours away. The small crowd round the bar where the payphone was located had created a false impression of numbers. They showed all the signs of having been there all day, of having no immediate intention of leaving. On the piss. Go on, Kev, just another one. At least Jacobson wasn't in that category yet. Kerr only half-consciously registered this distinction as he tried to untangle the implications of their mutual update. Ever since he'd followed them around Harvey's flat, he'd been convinced on the level of gut feeling that the Kents should be regarded as official contenders. Now, he thought, surely the only question was which one had planted the letter: who was implicating whom? The disguised, muffled voice on the incident room tape had sounded male to the untrained ear but you could never be sure until you got the expert analysis.

Jacobson put down his pint glass and spoke as if he was a mindreader.

'There's still nothing really puts Dr and Mrs Kent in the frame, old son.'

'Not much! Just a letter which shows that Roger Harvey and Annie Kent had been lovers since their student days and that John Kent *knew* what was going on: jealousy and rejection, the classic motives.'

'Ian! Ian! Let's keep it in perspective. If you've read his letter correctly, Harvey certainly looks to have been knocking off Mrs K without Dr K's approval. But on the other side of it, the three of them look to have remained friends throughout – so why should John Kent suddenly take it into his head to top his best mate at this particular juncture? As for Annie Kent, we realised when we started to look at Laura Gregory that the *modus operandi* doesn't rule out a woman. But think about what you've just told me yourself. The affair's been on and off for years. He even brings his other girlfriends round to tea! So why in God's name should she freak out now? I'm not saying we shouldn't be looking at them again, I'm just trying to talk in terms of the probabilities.'

Jacobson halted his assessment at the approach

of a bosomy, beehived, no longer young woman in a yellow micro skirt. Kerr couldn't work out if Jacobson was concerned about professional confidentiality or just liked what he saw. The woman smiled unsteadily at them as she negotiated her way through the sea of tables towards the Ladies. In her absence, her companion at the bar helpfully ordered another shot for her vodka and tonic. Kerr poured the last of the mineral water into his tumbler.

'By probabilities, you mean Mitchell and Gregory are still your numbers one and two, I suppose.'

'Exactly. Mitchell lives across the hall for fuck's sake – and he's seen with Harvey the afternoon before the murder which is also the day before he plans to skip the country with his company's software. All of a sudden, Mr Average is breaking the social taboos in a big way. Why stop at theft? He has a motive for jealousy as big as anyone's plus, unlike either of the Kents, it's all new to him, he's no track record of just putting up with it. Meanwhile, Ms Gregory's as jealous as they come plus she has a proven history of violence. Thanks to your chat with Merchant, we know she pulled the knife stunt on Harvey not once but twice and, thanks to young Emma, we can probably raise doubts about her alibi.'

Jacobson lit a cigarette and held it at arm's length so that the blue trails of smoke drifted in the opposite direction from Kerr's face.

'Apart from anything else, Ian, you still can't place either of them as anywhere other than snuggled up in their canal boat at the moment the culprit was bashing the dragon into Harvey's skull.'

Kerr lifted both hands in mock surrender. *Kamerad*! It had been Jacobson who'd pointed the finger at the Kents in the first place. The chief inspector could be a cantankerous old sod when the mood took him but at least he'd conceded that the Kents merited further investigation. The mineral water was luke-warm but he swallowed it anyway. It occurred to him again that all of Harvey's potential killers were united by a common motivation. If he hadn't put it about so much, Dr Roger Harvey might have been alive and well and sitting at his word processor. Jacobson moved the ashtray to the edge of the table, tipped his ash carefully. He seemed to read Kerr's thoughts a second time.

'Poor old Harvey, eh? Looks like no one ever bothered to speak to him about safe sex.'

Outside, it was the perfectly sunny day which forever endures above the cloud line but below them they could see the filthy-dark bank of rain moving out to the North Sea. Barber could anyway from his window seat but Mitchell and, even more so, Hume would have had to lean over in their seats to see very much at all. Neither of them looked especially bothered.

Hume was studying the details of the head-phone channels in the airline magazine. Periodically, you could see him hitting the buttons on his arm-rest with his left hand. To do this, he had to put the magazine on his lap and then pick it up again since his other hand was discreetly cuffed to Mitchell's. Probably they could have risked uncuffing him for the duration of the flight but this was a big guy: they'd decided not to take any chances. Mitchell himself just looked straight ahead. Whether he was gazing into the past or the future or felt himself stuck in the present it was impossible to say.

Barber replayed the meeting-cum-interview in his mind. It had been tough going all the way through but in the end they'd managed to sell him a bog-standard, implicit deal. If Mitchell insisted on a drawn-out, formal extradition he'd only be delaying the inevitable and would brand himself as 'hostile' and 'uncooperative' into the bargain. On the other hand, they'd suggested, there was always the possibility of leeway if he chose to cooperate. 'Your employer might even pressure us to drop some of the charges ultimately. Especially if you should find yourself in a position to return or restore their property. You'd be doing yourself a favour, mate, to get on the plane today and help us sort it out.' It was all true, he thought, it just wasn't all of the truth! The Harvey inquiry was another kind of animal altogether from the issue of computer theft. The biggest favour Mitchell could really have done himself would have been to sit tight in Holland and let the investigation run itself into the ground. The Dutch lawyer knew the game all right and had consistently advised him to stay put. You could tell from their faces that the Dutch questioned the ethics of it but none of them, not even the lawyer, had said anything. Bless their tolerant, liberal socks!

Barber's ear popped. They were starting to lose altitude, circling in for the landing. What was impossible to guess was why Mitchell *had* agreed. It was easy, straightforward, to understand if he wasn't the killer and didn't know what had happened to his erstwhile neighbour. But if he was the murderer then who knew what complex mixture of hope, fear and possibility had motivated him? Barber turned away from the window and studied their prisoner's face at close range. Still calm and collected: still no sign of what he might be thinking. Either way it would be instructive to see his expression again when Chief Inspector Jacobson revealed to David Mitchell what he really wanted to have words about.

The Dance Factory had taken over from the Crowby Martial Arts Studio which had taken over from Crazy Davey's Carpet Discount in the draughty hall at the rear of the red brick building which once upon a time had been the Crowby Tabernacle United Reform Church. Two women, one in gold lycra and one in green, were clambering exhaustedly into a shiny new Vitara as DC Smith turned into the customized car park. She glanced at Kerr and Williams and thought about Laura Gregory's record. There were times when even the bravest fish welcomed a bicycle. The three of them got out into the very last minutes of the rain and took the path around the side of the ex-church which the youngest of the faithful must have followed to their separate acts of worship.

The invitation was still inscribed on a slab of white stone above the archway. 'Suffer the little children to come unto me (Mark 10:14).' Emma barely remembered the grandmother who'd played the piano at something the ageing keepers of family lore always referred to as the mission, but now an image came to her of a dark sitting room, curtained against the sunshine outside, and of fat, wrinkled fingers on yellowing piano keys. A snatch of conversation came with the memory too, something about not letting the devil have all the best tunes. Williams offered her a penny for them but she didn't reply. The decline in traditional beliefs wasn't exactly a hot topic of conversation on the force and there was no time anyway. Kerr pushed the door open and they followed in after him.

Get up on your feet, get into the beat. The devil seemed to be getting it all his own way. The music faded and the late afternoon class settled into its mid-session break. Laura Gregory saw them as soon as they came in. She walked calmly over, wiping beads of sweat from her forehead with a white towel. The matronly woman at the hostel had only reluctantly told them where they could find her, had almost certainly contacted her after they'd left.

'Detective Smith! I wish I could say it was a pleasure.'

Emma had the warrant ready. It was an opening you didn't get every day, perhaps only got once.

'You do not have to *say* anything, Ms Gregory. But it may harm your defence if you do not mention now something which you later rely on in court.'

Chapter Nine

The note had been placed on the kitchen table next to a single rose. At first there had only been anger. He'd crumpled the paper in a tiny ball, chucked it across the room. Now he retrieved it, flattened it out, read it again, studying each word as if it was a hieroglyph to be decoded or as if each sentence might contain an oracle which could tell him how his future would turn out.

I think we both need the space to think things over so I'm going to stay at Marianne's for a few days. Don't worry – I won't be going into details with her, I know you think she likes to interfere. I just think that if we have some time separately we might be able to see where we're going, what we still want from each other. I'll ring you in a couple of days or you ring me. Sorry about last night.

Love, Cathy.

*

He picked up the rose and put it in a glass which he filled with tap water.

Vacantly he found himself checking every room out, seeking confirmation that she'd really gone. She hadn't taken much but the vital gaps in her wardrobe and in the bathroom cabinet were enough to convince him. He wondered if the familiar-looking red Astra crossing the fly-over just as he'd turned off the slip-road had been hers after all. Back in the kitchen, he tuned the radio on to the jazz request programme on Radio Three, catching the first bars of 'Freddie Freeloader'. It was almost an act of defiance, a declaration of independence. A true rocker, she'd never followed him into his mild investigation of the older music, teasing him for not keeping the faith, worse and inevitably, for starting to get old himself.

He mooched in the fridge and the freezer for a palatable, easily prepared meal and came up with a Marks and Spencer lasagne. Ian Kerr wasn't hungry, felt prey to a hundred emotions. DS Kerr needed to eat something, needed to be back at the Divi in less than an hour.

At the first bebopping notes, Alan Slingsby pressed the remote control and switched back to Kiri Te Kanawa on cd. He reprogrammed the selection to favour Verdi over Puccini and stepped, yawning, into the verdant landscape of his conservatory. It was his second weekend in a row without case papers to worry over. All the outstanding work was routine, could easily be handled by his junior partners. In theory, the situation was highly satisfactory. He'd invited Jill over to dinner and – if she stayed the night – then maybe they could drive out somewhere tomorrow, enjoy a late autumn walk if the weather allowed. Work *and* play. The balanced way of life. This had to be what it was all about.

Slingsby's bland, unremarkable features would probably still have adorned the non-competition, second dartboard in the Robert Peel Social Club had it not been for the curt memo from the chief constable himself. Slingsby and Associates were Crowby's serious criminal briefs, abrasive in court and adept in every technicality. Your paperwork or your procedures had only to be slightly smelly and Slingsby's clients were walking, giving you the one-finger salute on the civic steps as they waltzed out towards further self-help initiatives. More galling still from the canteen perspective was the fact that Slingsby himself didn't appear to be in it simply or entirely for the money. Part of his legend was that he'd been some kind of Maoist at university. As Barry Sheldon was fond of saying, you all know where that cunt's coming from. Amongst his other crimes against humanity, Slingsby had been known to waive fees in cases he regarded as deserving. He still gave free advice sessions in the neighbourhood law centres.

The phone started to ring in the short silence between two arias. The name Gregory meant nothing to him initially but the words Roger Harvey had been filed in the forefront of his memory since Thursday's lunchtime news. They dissolved his lethargy with the force of magic. He told the hotline clerk to tell the client he'd be there inside twenty minutes. It wasn't that he didn't want to spend the evening with Jill. Not at all. The concept was fine, it was just the practice of balance that he had problems with.

While Slingsby briefed Laura Gregory and Kerr and Barber rehearsed Emma Smith through her preparations for her first interview of a murder suspect, Jacobson spoke from his office to Professor Richard Elmwood in California. The telephone line was so clear he felt eerily that the American must really be hiding somewhere in the room. He'd only been able to speak to Elmwood's secretary the day before and it quickly transpired that she'd only known the least important half of the story. She'd known that Harvey had offered a paper to the American Historical Association conference, she'd known it had been accepted – she hadn't known about the job offer from UCLA's leading historical research centre.

'Well it was more than an offer, Inspector. There'd have been a formal interview when Roger came out here but we'd already sewn up the details between us. Tenure track, research grants, graduate support. Jesus! The guy was just hitting his professional stride—'

'And Dr Harvey had known about this for some time?'

'Oh sure. We tossed the idea around when I was out in Munich back in the spring but it was September before I was certain the faculty would buy it. I let Roger know straightaway. It must have been five, six weeks ago.'

Jacobson thanked him, cut the line and then dialled a number himself: the custody sergeant answered on a crackling, internal extension that might have been in Timbuctoo.

David Mitchell pointedly didn't look up when Jacobson and Barber entered Interview Room A a few minutes later. They both sat down opposite him and Jacobson stared into his unflinching, expressionless face. He offered him a cigarette – 'before we get started' – but Mitchell declined.

'You don't mind if I do then?'

'Yes, I mind. I'd prefer it if you didn't.'

Jacobson lit up regardless and puffed away, seemingly into space.

Far more was known about Sumerian astronomy, for example, than about their legal procedures. There would have been the usual amount of unjust and arbitrary punishments meted out by kings and overlords or at the behest of overzealous priests but, at street-level, it was likely that an acceptance of personal revenge provided the operational principle: you steal my wife or my sheep and I kill you, that kind of thing. An ancient Mitchell might have been expected, socially encouraged, to have a go at butchering an ancient Harvey.

Sometimes – when it worked – they got quite upset. Look, are you going to ask me any questions or what? Am I just supposed to sit here all day while you take your bloody rest-break? Before they knew it, they were telling you about the first time they went nicking in Woolworths, how many boyfriends their mother had, the moment when the iron first entered the soul.

A good three minutes passed before he fastidiously stubbed his cigarette out on the battered ashtray with its ludicrously inappropriate rim. Babycham, I'd love a Babycham. Mitchell had his feet planted, his hands clasped across his stomach. He hadn't even fidgeted but Jacobson supposed it had been worth a try. He'd been badly in need of a smoke anyway.

'Tell me about Sunday, Mr Mitchell. What you did, where you went, what time you got up.'

'Why Sunday in particular? I got up about eight as it happens. Had some breakfast, got over to Eschaton about quarter past nine. You can check the records.'

'And that would be when you tampered with the firm's software?'

'I've no comment to make on that.'

235

Mitchell's large frame didn't fit neatly into the dimensions of the narrow chair. Across the table, both Jacobson and Barber had the impression of looking at a caged bull.

'Tell me about later in the day then. You left work when?'

'Sometime after one. I've told you, they keep records.'

'And then what? Back to Coventry to see your wife perhaps?'

Mitchell still had his hands clasped but now each set of fingers started to play spasmodically up and down on the opposite knuckles. Mitchell was the only one who didn't notice.

'My wife isn't in Coventry. She's gone to what they call a New Age community up in the Lake District. Trying to sort herself out. We – we haven't been getting on too well lately. After I left Eschaton, I just went back to the flat. I can't see what any of this has got to do—'

'So you spent Sunday tidying up the flat, packing up?'

'If you mean, was I at the flat all Sunday, the answer is yes.'

'And you didn't go out at all, maybe call on a neighbour perhaps?'

The fingers went on kneading the flesh round the knuckles.

'Look, what's so important about Sunday? No, I didn't call on anybody. Yes, I was at the flat all day.'

'Let me get this straight, Mr Mitchell. You're saying you were there all Sunday after you left Eschaton and you didn't call in on any neighbours, none of them called in on you?'

'I've only been working here since August and I put long hours in. I haven't actually met any neighbours. It's just a place to sleep. I don't see why you're so interested in my spare time.'

Jacobson leant forward, resting his chin on the points of his thumbs, his elbows on the table.

'I take it you're suitably rewarded for your efforts? Nice house, car, sexy-looking wife. You work hard and you expect the dosh, the good life, right?'

'I've already told you about my marriage. I'm not money-mad, if that's what you're trying to suggest.'

'Of course not, Mr Mitchell, you were off to join the VSO when you ran into the Dutch police.'

Jacobson caught Barber's eye and nodded towards the door.

Barber crossed the room and rang the bell for the custody officers.

'OK, that's it, I've no further questions immediately.'

'So – what – I can go?'

'You can go back to the cells, yes. I'll speak to you later when I've made some further inquiries. I may want to tape our conversation at that stage. In the meantime we can arrange for you to see the duty solicitor or the custody sergeant will let you telephone your own legal representative if you have one.'

Mitchell waited impassively for the custody team to arrive, went out the room without uttering another word. Barber and Jacobson headed along the corridor in the opposite direction. The red light outside Interview Room B indicated that Laura Gregory's interview was still underway.

Inside the room, Kerr caught the exasperation on Emma Smith's face. He stood up, pressed his finger to the stop/eject button.

'This is Detective Sergeant Kerr suspending this interview at seven twenty-three pm.'

The tape clicked to a halt and he sat back down.

'Look, Ms Gregory, this isn't getting us anywhere. My colleague has asked you a number of entirely reasonable questions concerning your dealings with a man who's been brutally murdered and you've refused to answer nearly all of them.'

They'd given her time to change out of her dance costume before they'd brought her down the Divi. Now she was sitting across from them in designer jeans and a pink sweater. She looked warm and comfortable: just the ticket for a November night in the cells.

'How many times do I have to say this? You've charged me with two alleged attacks on

Roger Harvey so by law I'm fully entitled to say nothing about either supposed occurrence. As to what's happened this week, since it's got no bearing on either charge, again I'm fully entitled not to reply to your questions.'

Even complete idiots had kept quiet after Alan Slingsby's coaching. It wasn't surprising that someone like Laura Gregory was shaping up to be a star pupil. Kerr tried a different tack, abandoned his on-the-record manner.

'For Christ's sake, Laura, cut the crap. It might take time but we all know we can make the knife charges stick with or without your help. With your record, you're looking at another stretch. That's guaranteed. Not that we actually give a toss about a couple of minor lovers' tiffs. You know as well as I do that you're really here to help us with this week's business.'

He watched her draw a deep breath, keeping her cool.

'And by the way, Slingsby's misleading you if you think you can just clam up about recent events. Quite apart from the retrospective relevance to the charges we're holding you on, failure to help our legitimate inquiries into a serious arrestable offence – murder for example – that's chargeable in its own right.'

'But I've told you where I was, who saw me—'

Emma Smith cut in, shaking her head in a show of disbelief.

'Do you really think an English jury will buy

an alibi from a little tart like Wilkinson? I thought you were supposed to be an expert on sexism! The women will despise her and the men will all have hard-ons thinking about the things she gets up to – but not one of them will believe her.'

Laura Gregory looked away, retreated into silence. Kerr played his next card.

'If you really didn't do it, your only chance is to cooperate with us. If you tell us what you know, there might be something leads us to whoever did do it.'

He got up again and clicked the machine back on.

'This is DS Kerr re-commencing interview at seven twenty-nine pm. Present also are DC Smith and Ms Laura Fielding Gregory.'

Emma asked her again about Sunday night.

'I've already told you where I was and what I was doing. I wish to record that while this tape had been switched off, I have been subjected to both illegal threats and inducements by the officers present and that I fear for my physical safety in continued police custody.'

Somehow Kerr managed to keep the anger out of his voice.

'Ms Gregory's claims are absolutely untrue. We broke off the interview purely to give her time to collect her thoughts and consider her responses to earlier questions. Clearly a longer interval would now seem to be in her best interests. This is DS Kerr terminating interview at seven thirty pm.'

Jacobson was pleased to run into Sergeant Ince, the inquiry's uniformed liaison officer, when he got back to the incident room. Ince had been co-opted on to the anti-rave operation earlier in the day but appeared to have wangled his way back.

'Ince, old son! I heard you'd been dragged off to intimidate a hangar-full of acned students.'

'Along with half the force, sir. Fortunately someone upstairs still has a sense of priority.'

Ince was busy with the cuttings file. It wouldn't be the first case where somebody had talked to the press instead of the police but it didn't seem to be happening this time. Williams and Mick Hume were engrossed in the shopping centre security video which flickered muddily on a hastily acquired tv screen.

Barber and Jacobson grabbed a pew just as Williams freeze-framed on a dark-haired woman near an information kiosk and then let out a groan: magnified, if she was related to Annie Kent at all, she could only have been her granny. Jacobson stared gloomily as the camera panned for lost children and thieves, known or unknown. All his experience pointed to the contrary – Mitchell's lies had surely put him just where he wanted him – but some instinct or other still told him he'd played the interview all wrong.

*

John Kent found his wife in the bedroom, stretched out and dozing. At least, he thought, she wasn't foetally curled. He sat down carefully on the edge of the bed, making sure he didn't disturb her by his movement. He listened to her soft breathing: in and out, in and out. Saturday night stretched emptily before him. They wouldn't be going anywhere, doing anything. It was better to let her rest, she'd hardly slept at all last night.

Maybe he could finally make a start on the work he'd been planning since he'd got back from York. 'Your chapter on women, now that's of real interest.' He'd taken Wolheim's remarks as helpful – although he could see there was another interpretation possible – but he wasn't wildly optimistic. It seemed sadly late in the day to be jumping on the Women's Studies band-wagon. Now that even Crowby ran a degree, it was clearly an area which was well beyond its peak of fashionability. Wolheim had a point though; there was probably a solid enough little article to be cobbled together from Chapter Five. Play up the illegitimacy figures, births out of wedlock, talk about the barge women pursuing self-definitions beyond the confines of patriarchal discourse: the usual academic bollocks.

He still had the cold, sick feeling in his stomach. Work was probably a bad idea, even an impossibility. The television and another couple of stiff drinks sounded like a better bet. It wouldn't go on being like this. It was natural to feel like this now; for both of them. Sometimes it was as if your insides were cut up, lacerated. You wanted to grab hold of your guts before they spilled out of your skin. Other times, tonight, it was as if nothing in the world could ever be of interest again. Time would stretch on for a lifetime, then you'd look at your watch, see that less than five minutes had passed.

She was still asleep. He turned from the bed to the window, looked out across his well-worked garden, temporarily illuminated by the conjunction of a neighbourhood fox and their neighbours' too-sensitive security lighting. The crouching figure of Annie's Green Man stared up disinterestedly at him from the purposely wild shrubbery at the bottom end. Intermittently, he could hear the muffled slash of a chord sequence or a resonating blue note as the support band tuned up in the Wynarth Arms. It wouldn't go on being like this. You had to expect it for a while. It was only natural: but they'd get over it, come through it. He wondered if it would wake her up if he bent and kissed her.

David Mitchell hadn't enjoyed his first experience of incarceration either but at least the cell in Amsterdam had been clean. He rolled up his trouser leg and studied the flea which was silently munching at his mid-calf. He waited a few seconds before he pounced, trapping it between his left

243

thumb and forefinger. After a couple of failures, he'd finally evolved a workable technique. He eased the pressure off slowly until just enough of the tiny parasite became visible. Crrk! His right thumbnail spliced it in two with a satisfying crack. He flicked the tiny corpse on to the floor, noticed the red stain of his own blood which it had left on his victorious thumb.

Maybe, he thought, he should take up the offer of a solicitor after all. His first instinct had been to say no, not now. He'd wanted to get back here, to be on his own, to shut it all out. Watching that self-satisfied, pudgy face, the way his fat fingers had dab, dab, dabbed at the ciga- rette-end to put it out, he'd understood too late that the Dutch lawyer had been a hundred and ten per cent correct: he should have stayed right where he was and paid no attention to the rubbish about cooperation, leniency. It was up to them to make a case, not for him to convict himself. That fat, gloating face! But what could a lawyer tell him now that he hadn't worked out for himself? Exactly how many years he might spend in prison maybe. He wasn't sure that he wanted to find out. Prison! He knew that the reality of it hadn't begun to sink in yet, suspected that this was the mind's way of protecting itself from catastrophe, madness.

If he walked in a straight line, putting one foot close in front of the other, there was a grand total of eight and two-thirds steps he could take between the door and the furthest wall. Christ, he'd only wanted to live a little! Money-mad? Of course he was, who wasn't? One night when they'd had a few, Harvey had called it the *zeitgeist*, the new false religion. Too right! Except that there wasn't anything false about it. What the fuck else was there in life, in my life anyway? All those years of Jean spreading her misery, polishing her twin shrines to the dead kiddie and her doomed love affair. As if the boy's death hadn't hurt or wounded him at all, almost as if it was somehow his fault. As for her other obsession, well at least she couldn't blame him that she'd walked out on the great Roger. He hadn't forced her, hadn't even known her! He tried to think about holidays, nights out, the so-called happy times. Even when she did smile, laugh, it was always as if there was some last, vital ingredient missing. After some party where she'd looked and seemed on top of the world, you'd stagger awake at four or five in the morning, find her in the lounge with Van Morrison at full volume, an empty bottle of vodka lying beside her. *Astral Weeks*: that was what had made him start to wonder, rather than the coincidence of the first name. Harvey had suddenly taken to playing it three or four times a week. He'd first heard it wafting down the corridor late one night when he'd got back from a pub crawl with Brian Kennedy. Later on – when he'd finally had enough, was getting ready to make his move – he'd even asked Harvey to tape it for him, wound the bastard up about how his wife was a big fan too.

Six steps, seven steps, eight steps, turn. Six steps, seven steps, eight steps, turn. The whole mess was down to them. If they'd been more careful, hadn't carried on right under his nose, he'd never have done anything! Kolb had made his first approach in September and he'd told him to get stuffed back then, hadn't he? But that was before he'd known the score, before he'd decided to cut loose. Jean herself had given the game away. Every other Monday night for a month she'd phoned Harvey at his flat. Two sodding hours the call had lasted the second time. He supposed Harvey must have phoned her the other times. All very confidential, all very cosy. Except that then the stupid bitch heads off to Wacky Towers, leaves *him* to pick up the itemised phone bill. Mitchell almost smiled: it was so like her, always totally bloody impractical. Christ knows how she'd get on without him. Jean with Harvey, Harvey with Jean, Jean with Harvey. He tried not to see the pictures in his mind, tried not to hear what she'd said once, years ago, about the difference between the ways they fucked her, about there being no comparison. Six steps, seven steps, eight steps: he should have taken her apart there and then.

Six steps, seven steps, eight steps. He was just coming up to the turn when the custody sergeant opened the cell door. The figure just behind him was Jacobson.

'I want to talk to you again in a few minutes, Mr Mitchell, give you the chance to restart from scratch if you're smart enough to take it. You might want to read this first.'

The sergeant handed him the tattered but readable copy of yesterday's *Evening Argus,* the local paper, and then they were gone, the door shut and bolted.

He forced himself to sit down on the narrow bench, the one item in the room which was indistinguishable from its counterpart in Holland. For all he knew, they were identical in every police station in the world. Beijing to Brussels, Cairo to Crowby. For some reason the idea made him want to laugh out loud. He told himself to get a grip, realised he was close to panic, even hysteria. At least, he thought, read the thing all the way through. 'POLICE SEARCH FOR COUPLE IN MURDER HORROR FLATS HUNT.' There wasn't much detail to it but no doubt pudgy-face knew a lot more – or thought he knew a lot more – than he was telling the papers. The photo spread took up more space than the actual story. Harvey was on the left and he and Jean were on the right, the happy couple on the package-holiday beach. He tried absurdly not to catch Jean's or Harvey's eyes and then tried just as absurdly to pretend that he wasn't trying.

The fat, pudgy bastard! So that was why he was so concerned about Sunday, why his interest in the software scam had been so obviously shallow. Playing games, waiting for him to trap himself, trying to push him over the edge! You'd think he was a fucking terrorist or something. Footsteps shuffled. The door opened again.

'You heard him before, mate. He's ready to see you now.'

The custody sergeant led the way at a steady gait, his broad shoulders declining into a stoop. Hadn't they heard of early retirement round here? By contrast, the two constables to the sides and slightly behind him were hardly more than boys. The one on the left looked like he hadn't even begun to shave. He listened to the soft, padding echo of his shoes. They sounded slightly out of step with the black, polished thud made by his escorts. They made their way, a penitent's procession, along the hushed corridor.

It was madness. There were security cameras at regular intervals. As they approached the stairs up, you could make out the big red panic button. Madness. There was a camera above him right now. He was under arrest and in a bloody police station. Madness. He hadn't a clue which part of the complex of buildings he was in or how the layout related to the world outside. They'd taken away his trouser belt, would've done the same with his shoe-laces if his shoes had had any.

Madness.

He took leftie out immediately. Something cracked in the rib area when he elbowed him, then his right palm was flat under the bastard's chin, his left hand slamming the back of his head against the brickwork. He thought he saw something red slurring against the wall as the shaveless face slumped but then he was twisting his foot into the other one's balls, thinking better of a roundhouse kick to his skull and settling for a clean, solid punch to the jawline. He wouldn't be out for as long as leftie but he was out all right. The old boy was headed for the button. If it had taken longer to reach him, his resolve might have vanished. He might have come to, surrendered, ended up wiping leftie's head till help arrived. But it was only seconds, only madness. He tripped him, felled him, made it to the top of the stairs.

He expected the noise of running feet, whistles, sirens: but there was nothing. An office door was open, its interior empty. He crossed to the window, saw that he was on the first floor, somewhere at the back. There was a small car park below him. They weren't police cars so they must be the police's cars, the off-duty ones – their own cars, that's what he meant. The car park had an open entranceway which led on to a normal, everyday public street. In the distance a normal, everyday middle-aged woman was walking past with what looked like a pug on a lead. She was wearing a purple coat. It wouldn't be a comfortable drop but it wouldn't kill him. It was only madness after all.

He landed well enough, knees bent, frame relaxed for the impact. But the force of it still knocked him forward, dazed him for a few seconds. When he got up, he found he had to keep the weight off one ankle. There was blood on his forehead. He crouched behind the nearest car, then moved from behind one car to the next, always headed towards the entranceway. It was like something he'd seen in a film.

He touched the suffering ankle but the pain made him leap. Another crazy thought found him. It was no madder than the rest, no madder than the likelihood that he'd get this far. At the fifth car it worked: the unlocked door, the key in the ignition, the engine still warm. He would have expected the police to know better.

Chapter Ten

In the doorway of the hangar, Mel, of Posse Mel, had spent a stressed-up hour. He'd never felt entirely convinced that Crowby could be a cool venue, had let himself be swayed by the enthusiasm of associates. Now it seemed that he couldn't believe either his eyes or his luck.

'It's Mel again, Dave. Chill. It looks like the problem's gone away all by itself.'

He pushed the aerial down, stuck the phone back in his pocket. All the way along the pot-holed runway of the disused airfield, the police cars and vans were starting up and moving away like an army under sudden, urgent retreat. As they headed back to the main road, their various red, blue and yellow lights became more and more visible, captured by the very moment when evening gave way to night time. A big yellow moon rose up above the scalded clump of trees at the far edge of the runway. He tried to follow some thought about the moon and the car lights, something about motion through space, but he lost it in the relief that the party had been saved. He turned towards the door, grinning.

Crowby *was* cool.

It was incredible. It was pathetic. But at least, Jacobson thought, it wasn't their fault. They'd only brought Mitchell in; it had been the plods who'd let him escape. Even Sergeant Ince, hurriedly changed into civvies, could distance himself from events, allow himself the luxury of the scratched head, the grimace of contemptuous disbelief.

'Half a million quid on security cameras. All that monitoring equipment and nobody's looking in the right place at the right time.'

There'd be hell to pay, official inquiries, heads would roll – but there'd be no dirt sticking to the floor of the incident room. It was a situation in which you could afford to be philosophical, magnanimous. Mick Hume's was an unexpected voice of reason.

'What do they expect upstairs if they take half the shifts off their normal duties, even stick specials in roles they've never been trained for?'

Jacobson watched the faces, let the conversation run on. Young Ogden, still in his first bloody week, had taken a bad beating, would probably be seeing Christmas out in the General. There was anger here, outrage. It was better expressed before the operation than during. He

252

let another minute pass. Then it was time to get things moving.

'Listen up. I don't want heroics here. If we spot him, all we do is keep him in sight and call for back-up. Christ knows, the uniforms need a chance to redeem themselves on this one in any case.'

Jacobson, Ince, Smith and Williams would be in one car and Kerr, Barber and Hume would be in the other. Both would be unmarked, a roving additional presence to the big coordinated effort. As the team filed out, the shopping centre security video played on unheeded. Kerr, who'd been at the canalside only yesterday, had been as involved in the catch-Mitchell conference as everyone else. While they'd been talking, the clear, sharp image of Albert Peck had entered and left the Gents unobserved: with and then without Roger Harvey's letter to Annie Kent.

Ince followed an intuitive, random route, staying close to the heart of town but skirting the actual centre. Streets, houses, vehicles, people; Jacobson, like Smith and Williams, tried to scan every detail as it flashed by. Mitchell was resourceful, too smart to make any direct or immediate attempt to get out of Crowby. He was out there somewhere: around this corner or along that cul-de-sac.

He'd be lying low, thinking his way towards his next move. After the blind panic of escape, now he'd be all calculation, caution, reflection. The problem was there was no telling what mad, desperate actions his thoughts might lead him to. Shit! Even if they got him back soon, the plods had given the hierarchy the golden opportunity to stage their very own field day. There'd be wall-to-wall seminars on procedural management, audit trails, critical path walk-throughs. Well it was a plod balls-up and that was all there was to it!

His eyes strained across the crowd as they cruised past the Royal Oak where a bouncer-public altercation was developing nicely. The Oak had recently transformed itself into Drifters Nite Spot – mainly by the device of a big blue canopy which fluttered against the wind over the main doors. Now a couple of hanging flower baskets had been added on either side. The way things were shaping up down below, it seemed as if they'd be lucky to see their first night out. Shit! A plod balls-up was all there was to it! The uneasiness he couldn't pin down at the end of the interview had just been pure coincidence. What else could it have been? The look on Mitchell's face when they'd shoved the cover of the *Argus* under his nose was exactly what he'd expected! You had to use shock-tactics sometimes. His approach had been good, sound, effective. Shit! It wasn't his fault if the plods had fucked up!

David Mitchell had never really got the hang of

Crowby's traffic system, for some reason had never been able to hold the geography of the place together in his head. He turned the car into a quiet-enough looking street, parked cleanly between what was either a builder's or a plumber's van and a newish Golf convertible.

He'd lashed out in panic. That was all. He'd never really expected to get away, certainly not to get this far. What the hell was he going to do now? His ankle would barely take the weight of the clutch pedal, the cut on his head was still bleeding. Also he had no money whatsoever: not a penny, nothing. By the time he found his way to any of the through routes, there'd be road-blocks, checks. The poor bastard who'd left his keys in his car would have a red face – you had to laugh at that – but he'd also have the registration number, the detailed description. He was sure he'd already heard a helicopter overhead. Even if he had any money, the bus station and the railway station would soon be crawling with police if they weren't already.

Cautiously, he looked around him. It was a street of terraces on either side. Mostly neat and in good, improved condition. Handy for the centre of town too. Some bugger must have wheelbarrowed it to the bank on the proceeds when the property boom was at its height. A young Indian or Pakistani couple walked out of the nearest pathway, got into the convertible. Think normal, act normal. He looked straight ahead, watched them reverse and drive off in the mirror.

A white car paused at the top of the street. He froze, unable to move or think, but it passed on: a taxi not a police car. He cursed Jean and Harvey under his breath. It was their fucking fault he was in this mess. Fine, great, he thought: but now he *was* in it, what the hell was he going to do?

He got out of the car and locked it. He walked slowly along the pavement, maintaining a more or less normal gait at the expense of considerable pain. He clutched the car keys in his right hand as if they were still talismanic, could still transport him away from all his troubles. There was a telephone box at the top of the street outside a corner shop. It was one of the new, supposedly vandal-proof variety, all metal and a minimum of reinforced glass. The observation post: he stepped in quickly, ignored the protests of his ankle. He peered into the interior of the shop. There wasn't a single customer to be seen. Behind the till, a young girl, her hair in styling-kit ringlets, seemed fascinated by the screen of a tiny portable tv. No doubt there would be some-body in the back-shop but even so it would be the work of seconds, the easiest thing he'd done all night, to empty the till, get himself some ready cash. But then what? Tell me that: then what?

Almost absentmindedly he lifted the receiver, wondered if it was in working order. The message – the answer – appeared just to the left of the coin slot: 999 calls only. He put it back down, checked the interior of the shop again. It was still empty. He fingered the car keys, noticed for the first time in the phone box light that the fob was red leather. The enamel crescent held the wording and the symbol of the Crowby Lions Club. Only yesterday, the whole bloody world had been his oyster. Kolb hadn't been daft enough to tell him outright *who* he'd sold the DawnTrader system to but he'd hinted at a major player. Had to be anyway, Mitchell thought. The fee to Kolb and his associates and his own pay-off were the least of it. Only a company with real industry muscle would get away with re-branding DawnTrader as their own, would have the clout to hit Eschaton with a hundred writs in a hundred courtrooms if they so much as whispered a complaint. It had tickled Mitchell at the time. He'd looked forward to reading about it in the business section of some week-old English paper while he sank a cold beer at a beach bar somewhere a long, sunny way from Crowby. But that had been Friday and Friday was gone. Right now, tonight, his options had shrunk and vanished until finally there were no more than two of them left. He put the bunch of keys in his shirt pocket, suddenly noticed how cold he was feeling. There was still no one in the shop, no one in the street. Slowly, painfully, he walked back to the car, got into the back seat. He didn't bother to lock the doors.

When he woke up, the clock on the dashboard said five past eleven. It was time enough. He clambered into the driver's seat, turned the car and crawled it to the phone box. The steel shutters were down and padlocked outside Jarvis's SuperMiniMarket. The call took him barely two minutes to complete.

He anticipated a hard time, almost certainly a kicking. He knew they'd pay no attention to his 'conditions', his 'demand' that the one he'd already dealt with, Jacobson, the devil he knew, did the business. He knew he'd nothing real to bargain with anyway. They could put a trace on a call virtually instanteously these days. The area would already be sealed. The nearest packs of bully-boys would already be racing each other for the spoils.

He moved away from the phone box, struck by a ludicrous impulse. When the first police car swung round the corner, the headlamps picked out their objective immediately: David Mitchell, sitting on the bonnet of the stolen car, swinging his good leg backwards and forwards against the bumper.

Ian and Cathy Kerr lived in one of the Bovis houses which had been built off the Wynarth Road. When the traffic was quiet like it was now, you were only ten minutes from the centre of

Crowby in one direction, approximately the same from Wynarth in the other. Kerr pulled off the main road and stopped his car just inside the estate. He'd offered to go to the hospital himself but Jacobson had said no, he'd do it, everyone else could go home, the overtime budget was stretched as it was. He tried Marianne's number for the third time. Still no answer. He let the phone ring a good half dozen times before he cancelled the call. She would go there, he thought: Marianne of all people! She'd been plain Marianne when they'd first known her. Then she'd been Marianne-and-Geoff. Nowadays – Geoff having fled the coop with some woman he'd met on a sales training course – she was Marianne-and-the-girls. In his mind, he could just see Cathy sitting in Marianne's front room knocking back the g and ts, ignoring the telephone with Marianne's bitter encouragement. Earlier she'd have helped her put her daughters to bed. All night Marianne would have kept up her relentless and practised who-needs-them-when-they're-all-such-bastards propaganda. He tried the number once more, gave it ten rings this time, then wheeled the car back out on to the main road.

Fifteen pounds admission: with less than half an hour left in the late bar and the legendary Frogman Henry already back in his hotel, the guy on the door probably thought he was crazy, had probably taken a gamble that it would be less trouble to let him in than to keep him out. He saw her at a table with a crowd of friends, the idea flashing in his mind that it was the very same one at which Stevie R had positioned the Harvey-Gregory run-in.

Her first name was Rachel, he didn't know her second name. Somebody near to her, somebody known loudly as Charlie, bulldozed his way to the end of a complex joke, his punchline nearly buried in cat-calls, the thumping of bottles on wood. Kerr wondered if it was only in his imagination that she looked set apart from the group, distracted. He'd nearly made it to the bar when she intercepted him. Maybe she could get him something, she was just about to get a round in anyway. He helped her carry the drinks back to the table, put them down in the middle. Sorry, she told him, her friends were a bit out of order, most of them had been here all night. Look, maybe they could sit over in the corner – there was a table free – if he didn't feel like joining in.

It was his first glass of beer in weeks, something to be savoured. They watched the crowds drink up and dwindle until they were amongst the last die-hard half dozen. She'd been going on to a party later but maybe he didn't want to. He looked as if he'd had a rough day or maybe a rough lifetime. She lived quite near actually. Maybe he'd rather just go back there: talk, a glass of wine, whatever.

He thought about declining the offer – saw

himself driving back to Crowby alone, flattered, resolute – but he hadn't bargained on the smile she threw at him as they emerged out on to the street and stood below the late-night sky, the clouds motionless against the bright, clear moon.

There were still occasions when Jacobson had to read the riot act, make it his business to know whether some dinosaur or other had been playing Judge Dredd. But this time he knew he couldn't find it in himself to go by the book – despite the large, purple bruise on the left cheek, the deep contusions around the upper lip. After all Mitchell had made a direct exit from the first floor of the copshop and then – as the officers concerned would no doubt testify – he was a big man, it had been potentially a difficult re-arrest. Besides it was nothing to the state of young Ogden elsewhere in the building. Even the doctor was keen to let it go, had cloaked his assessment in professional ambiguity: 'There's nothing about the injuries inconsistent with a serious fall.' He pulled a chair over to the side of the bed, found himself speaking unexpectedly quietly, almost gently. That part of it was over, evened out. Maybe that was the notion or maybe it was just that there were other, bigger issues on his mind.

'The doctors want you to rest tonight, Mr Mitchell. That's good advice. When I come back tomorrow, we're going to have a long, strenuous conversation.'

Mitchell's eyes were blood-shot, unfocused. He'd been sedated too although the doctor had reckoned there were still minutes to go before it took its full effect. Perhaps he should just have left the whole thing to the morning but now that he was sure of it, had taken the time to think it through, he wanted to get the point over straightaway. He didn't fool himself that he was concerned about Mitchell or that he felt any kind of genuine guilt about the stunt with the newspaper, the drama it had set in motion. Mitchell's actions were Mitchell's actions just like Frank Jacobson's were Frank Jacobson's. What it really was: he had to hear himself say the words out loud to know that he actually meant them.

'You'll want to talk to me anyway, Mr Mitchell. You see, I think I know that you didn't kill Roger Harvey but I need you to convince me that I'm right.'

Sunday

Chapter Eleven

Jacobson returned to the Crowby General Hospital at eight o'clock the next morning. An hour later, he grabbed a cup of 'coffee' from the scuffed drinks machine in the main reception area on his way back out. Too early for the influx of Sunday visitors, he watched all there was to watch: the woman from the Hospital Friends League setting up her flowers and books stall. The bypass would be quiet too. It was simply a matter of meeting Kerr at the Divi and then they could start to wrap it up. The mugshots had certainly speeded the process. Even though neither was recent, you couldn't easily confuse one for the other. Mitchell hadn't hesitated anyway, hadn't seemed to have the slightest doubt about which one. Mitchell could be lying of course. But if he was they'd know soon enough.

Two plods were bolting the stable door when

Jacobson and Kerr came out of the Divi car park. Jacobson showed his ID and restrained himself from uttering the obvious sarcasms. They drove on in silence. It was hard to tell whether Kerr was absorbed in the details of the case or whether he had something deeper, more personal, on his mind. Jacobson decided not to mention the fact that there'd been no response from Kerr's home number earlier. He'd been about to drive over there, wake the sod up, when he'd finally called in on his mobile. As they approached the Flowers Street junction, they were overtaken on the inside lane by something black and expensive. No. It couldn't be. It was: SLY 1. Alan bloody Slingsby!

Jacobson slowed to half-speed, got to the lights just in time for them to turn red, watched the people's friend disappear out of sight around the corner. There'd been the usual slanging match when they'd dropped all the charges, invited Laura Gregory to go on her way. But ultimately Slingsby was a professional. He'd as good as told her to button it when she'd started to rant about wrongful arrest, unfair questioning. He knew as well as anybody that they'd played a careful, defensive game. They'd even had the police surgeon check her out – in the presence of a female officer – when she'd made her ad lib claims about police brutality. The only chink in the armour was the pressure which Smith and Williams had put on Jackie Wilkinson who wasn't Slingsby's client in the first place: in the second place, now they'd assured her that she'd been eliminated from the Clarence Street investigation, the young mother wanted nothing more than to be left alone.

Red changed to amber and he slipped into gear, eased off the brake. The bottom line, the clincher, had been the prospect of media attention. Jacobson hadn't so much as fed them her name but a complaint, especially a rejected one, would put both her and the refuge on the local front page. When they turned the corner themselves, Slingsby's car was only a blur in the distance.

The four of them sat round the kitchen table. It was Jacobson's first visit but Kerr had started to feel like a regular caller. Beatrice Webb would have gone to sleep with her mouth dribbling over his shoe if John Kent hadn't tricked her out into the garden. Neither of the Kents looked as if they'd been awake for very long. Jacobson managed not to mirror Mrs Kent when she lit a cigarette. Like Kerr, he declined the offer of tea.

'Please yourself—'

Kent poured out two cups, passed one to his wife.

'But maybe you'll get to the point of your visit then. My wife and I have had a hellish couple of days and we've got the funeral tomorrow. We'd hoped we could at least try to have a peaceful Sunday.'

There was no easy way to do it, no best way. Like an old-style executioner, Jacobson could only offer the solace of the quick, clean blow.

'I understand how you feel, Dr Kent. We're here because we need to see whatever prescribed medicines either you or Mrs Kent have about the place.'

'Are you crazy?! What the hell kind of jo—'

'I'm sorry. I'm not crazy and I'm not joking.'

Jacobson dug into his pocket, passed a form across the table.

'Here's the warrant duly signed by an appropriate magistrate less than half an hour ago. There're basically two things you can do. You can either show us where you keep any medicines or you can watch us struggling not to make a mess of your house.'

Kent picked it up, looked at it, probably didn't take in a single, official word while Kerr crossed the room towards an old chest of drawers which had been skilfully sanded, stained, varnished. There was a pile of bills and letters sitting on the top and a woman's shoulder bag, good leather. He never knew whether he really felt Annie's eyes burning into the nape of his neck in those moments or whether it was just his imagination. He fished inside and brought out two darkly-coloured pill bottles, each with a neatly printed, neatly dated label. He turned round, nodded his head in reply to Jacobson's silent question.

268

There was no easy way, no best way. Jacobson got up, stood between the table and the door into the hall.

'Mrs Anne Alexandria Kent. It is my duty to arrest you for the murder of Dr Roger Harvey.'

Do you wish to say anything? You're not obliged to say anything. He stuck to the precise form of words, told her she'd make a first court appearance in the morning. John Kent picked up a kitchen knife, grabbed his wife round the waist, told them to keep away.

It wasn't serious, he didn't mean it. They waited till he put it down, watched the tears well in his eyes behind his moon spectacles. Mrs Kent sat back down. They let her finish her cigarette, told him he could follow them to the station if he really wanted to. As they made their way along the hall, they could hear Beatrice Webb whining and pawing at the back door like an abandoned child.

Jacobson left Kerr to process Annie Kent into custody, took the creaking lift to his office on the fifth floor. He wanted to get the rough details down on paper straightaway; it would make life easier when he had to write up the official summary later. He opened the bottom drawer of his filing cabinet and considered in turn the jar of instant coffee and the full-size bottle of Glenlivet which he kept concealed behind his kettle and his brown-stained bag of sugar. Unable to choose between them, he did without either.

He'd never thought too much of Laura Gregory as a suspect but as recently as yesterday afternoon he would still have given top billing to David Mitchell. Even when he'd come to focus on the Kents, it had been John not Annie that he'd reckoned on at first. Harvey's imminent departure to Los Angeles, he'd thought, could well have been the last straw for him if he'd known about it or guessed.

Kent cut a sorry figure by contrast to Harvey: his career stuck in the stagnant pool of Crowby, his book a failure. Worst of all, his wife was going quietly bananas because another man had ditched her. He had a whole set of motives. The problem had been that, like his wife, he seemed to have spent the entire weekend on a canal boat. Like Kerr, Jacobson had initially dismissed Annie's lie about the Valium as a trivial mistake made in circumstances of understandable confusion.

But that had been before he'd paid his hospital visit, before he'd known that David Mitchell hadn't tampered with Eschaton's system on Sunday morning after all – that he'd actually done the business late on Sunday night with the help of a sizeable backhander to a CrowbyGuard security man. When he'd finally spoken to him, Mitchell hadn't seemed to care about any of it any longer, had just let the whole story rip.

'I heard music – that music – playing in Harvey's flat when I got back, realised he must still be up. I just couldn't resist calling in one last time, do a bit of gloating. If he'd been on his own, I think I might even have told him what I was up to. Anyway, he wasn't on his own. There was this woman there with him. Her, the dark-haired one, not the other one. I lost the rag a bit, I must admit, gave him some right old verbals. Whose slag's this one? Whose wife are you shagging behind whose back now? I just wanted to let him know that I knew, see? That I wasn't some clueless mug punter. I felt like hitting the bastard – I don't mind saying – but he wasn't worth it, not with a million quid up for grabs. Yeah, that's right, I slammed the door when I went. Left them to it, basically.'

Jacobson scribbled the main points down from memory. He would worry about collating the formal statements later. As far as he could recall, Mitchell's malevolent testimony tallied precisely with everything the Ahmeds had reported on the first day of the case. It was some consolation that Mitchell would certainly do a stretch for the assault and break-out: what would happen with the other charges probably depended on whether he could help Eschaton regain control of their product or not.

So Annie Kent had driven back to Crowby in the early hours. She'd pleaded with Harvey not to end their affair, maybe even asked him to take her with him to the States. She'd endured Mitchell's torrent of abuse but perhaps what she couldn't endure – finally – was Harvey's ability not to need her.

She'd told Kerr that her GP had prescribed Valium to help her cope *after* Harvey's killing but the date which Kerr had read on the two bottles he'd seen had been the 21st of October – a full month *before* the murder and only two days later than the date of the letter in which Harvey had tried to end their relationship. Valium on its own would just about have done the job after John Kent's three or four pints of real ale in the Castle Arms, but what Annie's doctor had ordered had been Valium *and* Mogadon. Float through the day and doze like concrete through the night – the traditional, increasingly unfashionable combination. After a nightcap of moggified whisky or decaf, John Kent wouldn't have known a thing about his wife's midnight excursion unless she chose to tell him later.

Jacobson believed she had told him, most probably after he'd noticed the missing dragon. He was sure he'd covered for her, would probably have incriminated himself if he could have seen a way to do it. Not that this speculation would find its way into the chief inspector's final report. Kent had already paid a penalty for his wife's crime, looked set to carry on paying.

He heard the clock strike eleven on the white tower of the town hall. He put his pen down, found himself gazing at the photocube of Janice and Sally which he'd never had the heart to remove from his desk. At least, he thought, there weren't any kids involved. His phone rang. It was Sergeant Ince. Ince had succeeded in gaining access to the Brewer's Rest ahead of opening time. The entire inquiry team was over there apparently: 'The rumour is you're buying, guv.'

Jacobson knew he couldn't stay long. Neither, he told them, could Ince nor Kerr. He restricted himself to a pint and a whisky chaser but he put a good show of notes on top of the bar to keep the party rolling for the others when he left. Ince drove them to the canalside in a brand new patrol car and at a grossly illegal speed. They got there only a few minutes after the diving team even though they'd left a good half hour later.

Albert Peck suffered several minutes of paranoia when he saw the police vans drawing up. Sergeant Ince, delegated to the task by Jacobson and forewarned by Kerr, explained to him what they were up to.

'Well, you've picked a fine day for it, Sergeant, I dare say.'

Peck watched Ince retreat back along the canalside. Now that it looked like he'd got away with it, he wanted to tell them what he'd done, how he'd helped them. But what would he do – where would he go – if it ended up costing him his job? You were always reading about folks who'd had a go but who'd ended up the worse for it one way or another. He decided to bite his tongue, contented himself with watching the final instalment unfold.

Ince rejoined Jacobson and Kerr on the bridge. The old boy was right. After the windy days, the rainy days and the windy-rainy days, it was the finest day they'd seen for some time. On either side of the canal, a small crowd of boat-owners gathered to watch the divers at work.

When you thought of all the vast space in the world which had no associations whatsoever for a particular individual, it never ceased to amaze Jacobson how often culprits settled for the tiny sub-set which you could associate with them: they found Harvey's dragon inside forty-five minutes, had to cover less than half a mile of water to do so. They also retrieved what were quite likely to be the sodden remnants of some of the letters which Annie had meticulously removed from his kitchen drawer.

Kerr could have stayed there all day. He had two phone calls or visits or decisions to make when he was finally forced to clock off. He didn't know which order to take them in, couldn't predict what he'd end up doing or saying. He watched the soco pack the dragon away for subsequent examination. Annie Kent had bought it as a token of love for a man she'd had to share but who'd been prepared to share her too. It had probably been as good an arrangement as any until one of the parties concerned wanted out.

Chapter Twelve

Afterwards

The London-Aberdeen InterCity had snaked into Crowby only three minutes behind schedule. Sally Jacobson was the tenth of the ten passengers who had alighted.

Unable to reach a more refined decision, they ordered a bottle of house white and a bottle of house red and decided to start with the white. He watched her raise the slim glass to her lips. Her hair was long again and blonde again. In a year she'd be the age Janice had been when he'd first met her. He was glad about the colour. If she'd still been wearing it black, the resonances with Roger Harvey's photograph of Jean Alison Mitchell would have been too close for comfort.

She told him about some of her recent work and the assignment she was travelling to. Newcastle-upon-Tyne, three days of location shots for a northern fashion house. It was funny, coincidental: he told her that was where his murder victim had lived before he'd moved to Crowby. She said she was sure she could break into real photojournalism soon. A guy she'd known at college was a youth worker in Wallsend. There was a chance of maybe doing something serious while she was up there. You know – streetlife, inner-city kids. Jacobson knew all right. He knew sights in Crowby which would have filled a hundred photographers' portfolios, momentarily disturbed a hundred thousand break-fast tables. But he said nothing about them, didn't say anything either about his fervent hope that somehow or other her career would get stuck in its glitzy beginnings, would never make it into what she probably thought of as the real world.

Their antipasti arrived just as Paul Morricone Junior himself announced tonight's Gala Surprise, music by the quartet led by none other than his own famous brother, Anthony Morricone. Famous was perhaps an exaggeration but Morricone's Jazz Express were certainly well known locally, even had an album behind them. Sally whispered that she'd seen them listed in *Time Out* earlier in the year when they'd attained the heights of a week's support residency at Ronnie Scott's. Not that jazz was her kind of music, not that Ronnie Scott's was her kind of place. Jacobson smiled an uncomplicated smile, didn't ask her what was.

He finished his glass then recharged both of them. Whatever their reputation really rested on, Morricone's band were sticking to the standards for tonight: crowd-pleasers for guests who'd come to eat and might – but might not – know John Coltrane from Madonna. Jacobson started to relax, even tapped his feet. Sally looked up from her plate. Her smile seemed genuine, uncomplicated, too.

By the time the main courses arrived, they'd drained the white. They'd finished off the red when the puddings put in an appearance. By that point, they'd already abandoned any idea of Morricone's authentic cappuccino and decided on Irish coffee, abandoned too their circling, guarded conversation about her ambitions, his work, the merely external circumstances of their lives. I'll have Drambuie and my daughter will have Cointreau. By then, she'd told him about Janice's curt postcard from the Bahamas where she was 'wintering' with Mackeson. To Jacobson's complete delight, she continually referred to his wife's lover as old sleazyballs.

He offered her a cigarette and took one himself. Both of them, and especially Jacobson, agreed that they'd be giving up in the morning. Definitely, certainly, no question. The Jazz Express were about to take a break but before they did so, they wanted to introduce their own special guest, a young lady they were sure you'd be hearing a lot more of. Jacobson leant back, briefly content in a comfortable chair, listened to the deep, smoky voice run through Cole Porter, Gershwin, Billie Holiday. She was a big girl too, a large lady, a big momma. He took a deep draw and blew out half a dozen perfectly blue smoke rings, something it hadn't occurred to him to do in years.

He smiled at Sally again, tried to think of a reason not to order another round of liqueur coffees or maybe just liqueurs on their own this time.

The Funeral Boat
Kate Ellis

A West Country murder mystery

When a skeleton is unearthed on a Devon smallholding, DS Wesley Peterson, a keen amateur archaeologist, is intrigued by the possibility that it is a Viking corpse, buried in keeping with ancient traditions. But he has a rather more urgent crime to solve – the disappearance of a Danish tourist.

Wesley finds disturbing evidence that the attractive Dane has been abducted. His boss Gerry Heffernan believes that Ingeborg's disappearance is linked to a spate of brutal robberies and that she witnessed something she shouldn't have. But is her disappearance linked to far older events? For it seems that this may not have been Ingeborg's first visit to this far from quiet West Country backwater...

'the abiding presence of history adds another dimension to this already intriguing tale'

Northern Echo

'moody mystery...a splendid piece of whodunnit, and when?'

Newcastle Evening Chronicle

The very best of Piatkus fiction is now available in paperback as well as hardcover. Piatkus paperbacks, where *every* book is special.

The prices shown above were correct at the time of going to press. However, Piatkus Books reserve the right to show new retail prices on covers which may differ from those previously advertised in the text or elsewhere.

Piatkus Books will be available from your bookshop or newsagent, or can be ordered from the following address:
Piatkus Paperbacks, PO Box 11, Falmouth, TR10 9EN
Alternatively you can fax your order to this address on 01326 374 888 or e-mail us at books@barni.avel.co.uk

Payments can be made as follows: Sterling cheque, Eurocheque, postal order (payable to Piatkus Books) or by credit card, Visa/Mastercard. Do not send cash or currency. UK and B.F.P.O. customers should allow £1.00 postage and packing for the first book, 50p for the second and 30p for each additional book ordered to a maximum of £3.00 (7 books plus).

Overseas customers, including Eire, allow £2.00 for postage and packing for the first book, plus £1.00 for the second and 50p for each subsequent title ordered.

NAME (block letters) _____

ADDRESS _____

_____

I enclose my remittance for £ _____

I wish to pay by Visa/Mastercard   Expiry Date:_____
